EXTINCTION HYMNS

"Eric Raglin's marvelous collection *Extinction Hymns* is a stunning patchwork of eerie tales that range from the bizarre to the somber and sorrowfully delicate. Moreover, this collection proves that horror is not merely one note. It is a magnificent symphony."

—Eric LaRocca, author of *Things Have Gotten Worse Since We Last Spoke and Other Misfortunes*

"Body horror melds with queer heartache and queer hope in *Extinction Hymns*. Eric Raglin leads us through melodically crafted strains of delight, despair, and desire. Both deeply human and wildly outrageous, his stories might save us through his unique brand of caring cruelty. He leaves us raw, yet somehow better than when we started."

—Joe Koch, author of *The Wingspan of Severed Hands* and *Convulsive*

"Raglin's aptly-titled collection is all about endings, from characters who bend and break themselves trying to stop them, to those who race head first into them. There's a through-line of destruction—of our world, others, ourselves—in *Extinction Hymns*, but also beauty in the uncomfortably familiar desperation."

—J.A.W. McCarthy, Shirley Jackson Award nominated author of *Sometimes We're Cruel and Other Stories*

Extinction Hymns

by Eric Raglin

Brigids Gate
PRESS

Content warnings are provided at the end of the book

CONTENTS

SILVER DOLLAR EYES

(First published in *What One Wouldn't Do*)

The name "Tuva" cut through the static. A girl's voice: high-pitched, lilting, and far too young to be dead.

In the dim glow of my penlight, I watched the tour group's reactions. The young daughter backed away from the spirit box. The mom squeezed the girl's shoulder, an attempt to comfort that instead made the girl wince. The dad donned a neutral face, but his toe-tapping gave away his nerves. It was only the teenage son who seemed genuinely unafraid. The boy stared down at his phone, its light disrupting the ambience. But I'd dealt with kids like him before and knew how to get their attention.

"Tuva," I said. "Use the energy from his phone to manifest yourself."

The boy frowned at me and stuffed his phone in his pocket. I grinned, rolling my wheelchair back toward the wall of my living room.

"Let's make space for her," I said. "She normally appears by the coffee table. Tuva, can you do that for us?"

The mom took cover behind my purple armchair, and the girl hid behind her. The dad stood between the living room and kitchen, hands pressed into the door frame as if it were threatening to close in on him. Even in the dim light, he looked sweaty. I glanced at the boy.

"If you feel cold, it's because she's right next to you," I said.

He brushed his arm as if swiping away an insect and squirmed backwards. I resisted the urge to laugh.

"Here," I said, rolling forward and placing my penlight on the carpet. "Use this, Tuva."

All of us watched the glowing light—the family for the first time and me for the hundredth. I knew what would happen, what always happened.

A flicker.

A gasp from everyone but me.

Darkness.

Then, a voice bubbled into existence, a child's cry both liquid and piercing.

"Tuva!" it said.

Scarcely taller than the coffee table, the spirit's form coalesced like a column of smoke. The fabric of her T-shirt rippled slowly as if caught in a celestial wind, and her eyes shone like silver dollars.

Everyone in the tour group screamed and bolted out of the room. The boy hurdled over the armchair to avoid passing through the spirit. And despite being the last to leave, he didn't close the front door behind him.

Only after they were gone did Tuva dissipate—an invisible resident once more.

The family wasn't coming back, but it didn't matter. I'd gotten their money, and they'd gotten more than they bargained for. Few would believe their account of what happened, but those who heard it would come to me, just in case.

"Good job, girl," I said, fingering the wad of twenties in my pocket. Cash was always my preference. Pleasantly tactile and harder to tax.

I turned out the penlight, cloaking the room in darkness. Seconds later, headlights spilled through the curtains, briefly illuminating the room before the family's car screeched away.

In the corner of the room, the floor creaked under the weight of nothing.

"Tuva."

Her voice was faint, defeated. She sounded like that more often lately.

"What?" I asked. "You want your cut? Not sure how much good cash will do you in the—you know, wherever you are."

"Tuva," she said again.

Always and forever "Tuva."

***

A year before that tour, I was working a construction job when an I-beam slipped and my legs met an early death. I sometimes joke that my house gained half a ghost that night. Sure, my legs still pumped blood, but they were dead in the practical sense—Tuva's new spectral companions. I imagined my ghost gams propping themselves up by the fireplace, pacing the kitchen while cookies baked, and doing morning hamstring stretches.

These imaginings were strangely calming, but they didn't change the fact that I'd be in a wheelchair until the day I died. No amount of physical therapy could get so much as a toe twitching. Not only that, I was out of a job. I'd never been one to have nightmares, but suddenly I was plagued with ones about overdrawn bank accounts, foreclosure notices, and nights spent homeless in the bitter Colorado winter. I often woke up shaking with no one to comfort me. No one but Tuva, that is. Not that a little dead girl who spoke only one word and slammed cupboards could do much for me.

We'd occupied the same house for three years but hadn't really bonded. Hell, I'd only mentioned her existence to a few people— none of the guys at work, of course. They wouldn't have believed me, but I couldn't blame them. I barely believed it myself the first time I saw her standing motionless in the living room. The landlord had never mentioned this little quirk of the house—big surprise there. After I got used to Tuva's presence and it no longer frightened me, I'd mention her to my matches on Grindr. "My house is haunted" turned out to be a great pickup line. Too bad most men ghosted me—no pun intended—when they saw my wheelchair.

Tuva couldn't save my love life, but she became my cash cow when nowhere would hire a man on wheels after fifty-plus job applications. I posted the first ghost hunt ad just as the leaves started to crisp and the thought of Halloween began entering people's minds. "THIS GHOST GIRL WILL HAUNT YOUR DREAMS," it read. Tour groups came in droves, and like that, my money problem vanished.

But no good thing lasts forever. My legs hadn't. My construction job hadn't. My friendships with former coworkers hadn't. Why the hell would this be any different?

***

I was four months into running ghost hunts when Tuva suddenly went dormant: no shouting her own name, no apparating beside the coffee table, no pushing books off the nightstand. Nothing. Having lived with her so long, I could feel her presence in the room that night, but the tour guests—seven members of the US Olympic ski team—didn't seem to notice. After two hours of exploring the first floor and basement without any paranormal activity, the athletes grumbled on their way out the door. One of them—a guy whose coat probably cost more than my entire wardrobe—was bold enough to ask for a refund. I coughed up the cash, knowing it'd cause more trouble if I didn't, though I sure could've used the money. The blood clots in my legs needed some expensive medical attention.

Seven tours passed without any paranormal activity. I realized that if Tuva wasn't going to play her part, I'd have to make up for it with engaging storytelling. Perhaps guests would still leave disappointed at the lack of supernatural spectacle, but a well-crafted tale would satisfy them enough that they wouldn't ask for their money back. I did some internet research on the history of my house, seeing what I could dig up about the girl and her death.

After hours of sifting through digitized land records and newspaper archives, I stumbled upon an obituary for Ingrid Birke, a five-year-old child who'd died of cancer a decade ago. I would have kept scrolling had the accompanying picture not looked exactly like Tuva. Skimming the obituary, a sentence caught my attention: "Ingrid is survived by her mother Laura and her sister Tuva." *Tuva.* Immediately, I opened a new browser tab and searched up "Tuva Birke from Denver, Colorado." Google Images displayed a woman in her twenties with close-cropped blonde hair and clear-frame glasses.

A voice cried out behind me, louder than I'd ever heard it before. Tuva's. No, *Ingrid's.* I'd been calling the spirit her sister's name the whole time.

"Tuva!" she said, and her ethereal form rippled like a disrupted reflection in a pond.

She repeated the word louder and with greater intensity again and again until my ears rang. I turned off the computer, the real Tuva's image banished to black. But Ingrid didn't stop. She'd seen her sister and couldn't unsee her.

I didn't sleep that night, haunted by both the dead and the living.

∗∗∗

Tuva Birke wasn't hard to find. Turned out she worked as a real estate attorney in Denver. I called the firm to be sure and was met with a "she's busy at the moment—may I ask who's calling?" I should've left a message, but … well, I couldn't. I wasn't sure why.

Ingrid's activity had become stronger than ever, as if her dormancy had been a way of saving up paranormal energy for later. She came out during the daytime now, and that wound up being the perfect marketing opportunity. My "Daylight Frights" ghost hunt proved popular with locals and tourists alike.

I remember one 2 p.m. tour especially well. Among the group of ten was some asshole who wore sunglasses on the back of his head and smirked more often than he smiled. We were ten minutes into the tour when Ingrid knocked over a chair in the dining room and appeared beside it, practically opaque. The man went wide-eyed and swatted Ingrid's form. The other guests gasped. Ingrid yelped and vanished.

"Holy shit!" the man said, inspecting the room for hidden strings or hologram projectors. "How'd you pull that off?"

"Don't touch her," I said, my jaw tense.

"What? Oh right, don't want to mess up the special effects."

The other guests bit their lips and stared at their feet. I took a deep breath. The man's accusation of fraud didn't bother me as much as the way he'd manhandled Ingrid. Truth be told, he hadn't been the first. How many times had I scolded guests for touching Ingrid, throwing things at her, or calling her names like "creepy little freak" and "ghost bitch?" Bile rose as I considered how Ingrid must feel, but I swallowed it, steeling myself for the rest of the tour.

That night, I got into bed without bothering to undress. The day had brought in six tours, forty guests, and eight hundred dollars in cash—a hell of a better paycheck than bricklaying ever provided. I'd be able to afford my thrombectomy soon. But that little peace of mind and my physical exhaustion weren't enough to put me to sleep. I stayed awake thinking about Ingrid. How much longer would she have to put up with people like that backwards sunglasses man? How much longer would she have to put up with me?

***

I paid for the thrombectomy two months later. The bill wiped out everything I'd saved, but being broke was better than dying of a blood clot. Still, I had a mortgage to pay, so I started booking tours the second I was released from the hospital.

That was when Ingrid went dormant again. I could barely feel her presence this time. It wasn't like she was easing her way into the afterlife but rather like she was vanishing from existence entirely. The tour guests started grumbling and demanding refunds once more. My storytelling couldn't make up for an absence of the promised spectacle. All it took was a few scathing online reviews to drop me from thirty tours a week to just five. My mortgage bill loomed over my dwindling bank account like the shadow of a mountain.

Desperate and drunk, I pulled up Tuva's picture on my computer again. When Ingrid failed to appear as she had before, I called out to her.

"Look, Ingrid, it's your sister," I said. "See? It's really her. Come back now, please. Please."

A small depression appeared on my mattress, but otherwise Ingrid stayed invisible. She knew what I was doing. Hell, I knew, too—but what other choice did I have? I sat there pleading with my product.

***

Ingrid's dormancy outlasted my bank account. Soon, all I had to my name were a bottle of bottom-shelf whiskey, a FINAL WARNING bank notice, and a blood clot back for round two. I pictured myself sleeping in a cardboard box, nestled between a stinking dumpster and a growing snow drift. Whether the cold or blood clots would kill me first was anyone's guess.

I drank. Drank and said some ugly things—not to the bank manager but to Ingrid.

"I'll kill your sister," I told her one night, whiskey hot in my gut. "I'll slit her throat if you don't show up for the tours."

Ingrid gave no response. She must've known I didn't mean it, or if I did mean it, that I couldn't make good on the threat. With two bum legs, I could get myself dressed just fine, but murder was a stretch.

Still, my barrage of threats continued until I passed out with a half-empty bottle in hand.

I awoke the next morning drenched in piss and spilled booze. My phone showed a missed call from the bank, but there was no need to listen to the voicemail. I groaned and rolled over, the late-morning light boring into the back of my skull. When I blinked to clear my eyes, Ingrid was standing beside my bed. Given my threats, revenge seemed as likely a reason as any for her return.

"I'm sorry," I said, squirming toward the far end of my double bed. "Please don't hurt me."

I couldn't read Ingrid's silver dollar eyes. Perhaps she was judging me, as well she should. Or maybe the dead left judgment to their gods.

Ingrid and I stared at each other for a long time. When she didn't move in for the kill, I realized this could be the moment my luck turned around—the moment that proved I wasn't a scammer. I reached for my phone. As I pulled open the camera app, I imagined the post I'd write online: *after a dramatic absence, the terrifying ghost girl is BACK! Book your tour TODAY!*

But when I lifted my phone to capture her, Ingrid vanished. I'd only ever see her one more time.

***

The repo men knocked on my door for ten minutes. I didn't have to look through the peephole to know it was them; the bank made it abundantly clear who to expect that February morning. I pressed the pillow over my eyes and tried to sleep through the knocking. No way was I going to make it easy for those bastards. They'd have to pull me out of bed and toss me in the icy streets themselves. I'd make sure they knew to throw my wheelchair out too.

The knocking got louder, and the man behind the door spat a threat that I couldn't make out with the pillow around my ears. The noise wasn't helping my hangover.

"Scare him off, Ingrid," I said. "You've scared plenty of people before. Don't want to get rusty."

I lifted the pillow to see if she'd made an appearance. Nothing. A groan escaped me.

"Alright, your choice." The repo man's voice was clear now without the pillow blocking it. "Cops are coming."

"Fuck you, man," I said, though I'm not sure he heard me.

Acid rose in my gut, and I pulled myself to the side of the bed. Hot, watery vomit splattered the wood floor. I'd let the repo man take care of that too.

Again, I glanced around for Ingrid, hoping she could save me as she had long ago, but she was still nowhere to be found.

"Fuck you, too, Ingrid," I said. "This is your goddamn fault for not—"

I couldn't finish the sentence. The words tasted even worse than the vomit—like a ball of shame, thick and fermented. I swallowed it. Tears came up in its place. I bit my knuckle to stifle a sob. As much as I wanted the repo men to take pity and stop the process, I couldn't bear to let them hear me like this. But I could hear them loud and clear.

"These fucking leeches," one said to the other. "Always making our job difficult."

I cleared the tears from my eyes and inhaled what felt like a dragon's breath. My mind wandered to the pistol in my nightstand drawer. I didn't know whether to use it on myself or the repo men. I opened the drawer, grabbed the gun, and clutched it like a prayer.

That was when Ingrid appeared in front of my bed, her form no longer translucent and rippling. She was as opaque as any living person. The only clue hinting otherwise was her voice, still half-underwater.

"Tuva," she said.

I stared at her, biting my lip until it bled, then gradually released my grip on the gun. Red and blue lights danced in the window. The cops were here, and they had no problem with making a show out of this repossession.

I remembered that Tuva was a real estate attorney. It wasn't clear whether she defended tenants or landlords, but my chest fluttered at the possibility that she might be able to help me. And Ingrid, too.

I let out a long-held breath and nodded.

"Okay," I said. "Tuva."

Ingrid's facial expression stayed neutral. Perhaps she didn't believe me. And why would she?

But I put down the gun, looked up Tuva's work number, and dialed it, hoping beyond hope that she was working today.

***

"This lady showing up any time soon?" a cop asked, squinting at me through the window. "You better not be bullshitting us."

"Yeah, could you maybe let us wait inside?" a repo man added, rubbing his red hands together and warming them with his breath.

I shook my head, searching the men's faces for any hint of shame. Mostly they looked half-frostbitten—an acceptable compromise.

Fairly certain they wouldn't break down the door before Tuva arrived, I left the front room to splash water on my face and change out of my vomit-soaked shirt.

When Tuva's car pulled up, it didn't look how I expected. I associated lawyers with money, but Tuva drove a sedan old enough to be a beater but not old enough to be vintage. Stepping out, she hesitated when she saw the house she'd lived in up until Ingrid died.

I told Tuva about the foreclosure over the phone but never said anything about Ingrid. Didn't even mention that I knew their mutual connection to the house. Tuva's impatient tone changed as soon as I mentioned my address. She paused for a long moment, then said she'd be right over to help.

"Little late for a lawyer, isn't it?" one of the cops said as Tuva approached.

Tuva didn't reply or even make eye contact. She looked at the house as if it were a mausoleum.

I opened the front door, rolling toward the wall so Tuva could come in. She hesitated at the entrance—a portal to pain. It was a portal for me too, but the pain existed on the opposite side.

"Thank you for coming," I said.

"Yes," Tuva replied, her voice as distant as her eyes.

I closed the front door, concerned that Ingrid might suddenly appear and turn this private reunion into a public affair. That moment didn't belong to the repo men and cops. It didn't even belong to me, really.

I cleared my throat, which still tasted like stomach acid. Sunlight glinted through the windows and magnified my hangover headache. I needed water and Tuva needed space.

"I'm thirsty," I said. "Can I get you anything too?"

"Sure," she said, trancelike as she scanned the living room. "Water."

I wheeled into the kitchen.

"Tuva!"

The word I'd heard a thousand times before took on new strength, no longer sounding like a voice from the bottom of the sea. Tuva gasped and fell to the floor behind me. I didn't turn around. This conversation belonged to the long-separate sisters, not to me. I rolled toward the faucet, grabbed two glasses, and filled them up. But the sisters' conversation cut through the hiss of water. I sat there listening, even as the cups overflowed, cold water spilling down my fingers.

"Oh my god, Ingrid. You're still here. How—? I … I thought we'd have more time," Tuva sobbed. "It's why I didn't drop out when you got sick. I thought if I could make it through the semester, we'd have all summer together and … and maybe you'd get better and we could … could climb Pikes Peak together. We always said we'd—"

"Tuva," Ingrid whispered.

In the reflection of the water glass, I watched Tuva lean in close. Ingrid whispered something in her ear, too quiet for me to register. Perhaps it was a message, a secret, a confession. I feared

Ingrid was telling her sister every horrible thing I'd said and done to her. All the humiliation I'd put her through with each tour. Maybe if Tuva knew the truth, she'd refuse to help stop the foreclosure. Not that I believed much could be done. And not that the foreclosure was the only reason I'd asked her here.

I sat at the running faucet with my eyes closed, trying not to think about how different my life might be an hour from now. I focused on the black space between thoughts like the emptiness between stars, hoping I was far enough away to escape their gravity.

I don't know how long I stayed like that, but a hand on my shoulder jolted me back into the present.

Tuva stood beside me, gray rivulets of mascara running down her cheeks.

"Thank you," she said.

"Don't," I replied, not out of modesty but out of genuine discomfort.

A knock on the front door, persistent and booming.

"Are we done here?" the cop asked. "A last-minute lawyer isn't going to change anything. You had your day in court and the court made its decision."

Holding back tears, I turned to Tuva.

"He's right, isn't he?" I said.

Blushing and blinking rapidly, Tuva looked away.

"Just tell it to me straight," I said.

She opened her mouth and said nothing for a long moment. Then, in barely a whisper: "I'll give you a ride to the shelter."

***

It would've felt good to confess the horrible things I'd done, but Tuva was harboring her own guilt. From her point of view, she'd given false hope that my house could be saved and now she owed me. Not that I agreed.

"I've got lawyer friends with housing connections," she said, dirty slush splashing the underside of her car.

I watched my home disappear in the rearview. The cops had done their job of getting me to leave, and now it was only the repo men going in and out of the house. Already, a careless pile of furniture formed on the curb. It'd probably be shipped to the dump before the end of the day.

"You won't have to stay in the shelter long, I promise," Tuva added. "I'd let you stay with me, but—"

"Please, no," I said. "You don't have to explain."

Tuva nodded and turned at the stoplight. My house was no longer in view. For all I knew, that'd be the last time I saw it.

Shivering, Tuva turned on the heater. Lukewarm, vinegar-smelling air poured from the vents. I stared out the window, watching the residential buildings give way to commercial ones and then vacant, fenced-up lots. We'd arrive at the shelter soon.

"Thank you," Tuva said, and again, I bristled at her gratitude. "I never thought I'd see Ingrid after—"

She sniffled, not just from the cold. After collecting herself, it looked like she'd continue with the thank-yous, but I couldn't let her.

"I ran ghost tours for a while," I said. "Ingrid made me a lot of money. When she stopped showing up, I … well, I didn't treat her very well. I knew she wanted you. But how could I give her up when …"

I gestured at my legs. Here I was justifying my cruelty in the middle of a confession. I resisted the urge to punch the glove compartment.

But Tuva only swallowed and nodded. Her car slowed to a stop at the shelter. Groups of women and children huddled together outside, waiting for the doors to open for lunch. There was also a man like me, wheelchair bound and a couple decades my senior. Puffy black patches of frostbite lined his nose.

"We'll be in touch," Tuva said, parking the car. "You won't be here long."

She got out first, opening my door and getting my wheelchair ready. I stared at her, desperate to read her eyes though they never met mine.

My wheelchair rattled in a gust of frigid wind, and I pulled myself into it from the car. Tuva grunted as she hauled me out of the snow and onto the shoveled but slushy sidewalk. As soon as she got me in place, she returned to her car, wordless, her head hung low. She pulled away, becoming a blue speck on the gray horizon.

I sat in my wheelchair and listened to the people around me. An old man mumbled to himself, a toddler cried to his mother, and a shelter volunteer peeked her head out to ask that we "please form an orderly line."

Winter wind cut through my bones, colder than I'd ever felt before. Colder than Ingrid. I hoped the girl had found peace: her connection to me severed, her closure with Tuva obtained, and her consciousness purged into nothingness. I was no longer her villain, but I wanted to follow her. Right into the bliss of oblivion.

THE RESURRECTION DOLL

The image is out of focus, but it's obvious Isaac is about to break character. His scene partner, Tom, stares at him with eyes wide as Saturn's rings. He's supposed to be the principal "disciplining" a naughty student, but his face—with all the subtlety of a silent film actor—oversells the sternness. Isaac's lips puff out, unable to contain the laugh that will soon make the director yell, "Cut, goddamnit."

This blown-up photograph is mounted above the bed Isaac and Tom shared for twenty years. Each night, Isaac stares at it until his eyes ache and his body shuts down. The left side of the bed is empty, but the sheets aren't cold. He wishes they were so he could pretend Tom's ghost was there. How comforting it would be to shiver the night away.

Isaac doesn't act in porn anymore, but he filmed enough scenes to catch gonorrhea in the worst of times and meet Tom in the best of times. Tom kept performing up until his death, even winning a GayVN for Best Oral Scene. It was funny watching his husband accept an award for sucking another man's cock, and even funnier when Isaac cheered the loudest of anyone in the crowd. He was sincere, too. When Tom dedicated the award to "the love of my life, and no, I don't mean Johnny Pound," Isaac happy-cried.

He revisits this memory as if it'll vanish the second he stops thinking about it. But Tom's slow dimming is inevitable: the shared closet no longer smells like his cologne and the VHS player ate the tape of their Joshua Tree wedding. To make matters worse, Tom's mother has stopped checking in. Maybe talking with her dead son's husband hurts, or maybe she blames him for Tom's death. Whatever the reason, her silence makes Isaac feel all the more distant from Tom.

But unwilling to let his husband disappear, Isaac finds a new way to preserve him.

***

The hyperrealistic sex doll arrives on a lonely Friday night. Isaac worked closely with the manufacturer to get the look just right, so the doll is more a custom art piece than a sexy silicone dummy. Its design is a composite of images taken from Tom's home videos, photo albums, and Facebook posts. Its face captures thirty-something toned Tom and fifty-something gaunt Tom, overserious porn actor Tom and dry-humored party host Tom.

Opening the box, Isaac finds the doll reflects Tom's many sides, but something is missing. His gut instinct is to put the doll back in the coffin-sized box and return it to the factory for alterations. But what would he tell them to change? The doll looks exactly as he specified. Maybe he's imagining imperfections that aren't actually there—a skill he's practiced often with himself. After a few minutes of deliberation, he decides he won't return the doll, at least not yet. It's best to sleep on the decision.

Not ready to call it a night, he gently lays the naked doll in bed, trying to determine what could bring out more of Tom's essence. A minute passes before he realizes it still smells like fresh factory plastic. He grabs Tom's cologne bottle from the mirror cabinet and spritzes the doll liberally before nuzzling its neck and inhaling. But there's little comfort in the act; the doll has no body heat, no moisture.

Tom used to sweat like every room was a sauna, glistening even in the dead of California winter. Isaac microwaves some wet towels, then drapes them over the doll as wisps of steam drift toward the ceiling. After a few minutes, he cuddles up to the doll again. The scent, heat, and wet are all there, but the recreation still feels incomplete.

Isaac holds back tears. He can't let this setback get him down. He'll try something else tomorrow.

Two sleeping pills and earplugs. He slides into bed beside the doll, which has cooled to room temperature, lifeless as ever.

***

It's 3 a.m. and the sleeping pills have failed Isaac, so why not ask the doll a few questions? A stupid game of make believe, but less fun, more therapeutic. When his questions go unanswered, he feels like a police detective interrogating a stubbornly silent suspect. Maybe he'll eventually break the doll down and get a reply.

"Why'd you make me drag out the stepladder to cut you down?" he asks. "Why didn't you leave a note?"

An edge creeps into his questioning. His hands tremble with repressed resentment. Before he can stop himself, he slaps the doll's chest. The blow leaves no red handprint, which only makes him angrier. His next slaps are harder, echoing inside the doll's organless frame. The hollowness reminds him that this thing isn't a flesh and blood human—isn't Tom. The doll resists Isaac's play pretend at every turn.

Whenever Isaac and Tom fought, they'd always iron out their differences with a good, angry fuck. Still conditioned for it after six months, Isaac hardens. He flips the doll over and shoves his cock in its ass dry. He thrusts with a vigor that borders on violence. Spittle clings to his lips. His eyes bulge. He climaxes within seconds, and tears immediately follow.

"I just want to know why," he weeps.

But sleep takes him before the answer comes.

***

When Isaac wakes up, the doll's asshole is bleeding. The blood couldn't have come from his cock, crusted only in last night's semen. Maybe the dry pounding tore up the doll's insides and spilled some weird synthetic liquid. Even though it isn't actually Tom, Isaac feels guilty.

"I'm sorry about last night," he says, cleaning the doll's anus with a wet wipe. "You deserved better."

The liquid keeps dripping, as slow and viscous as honey from a tipped-over jar. Isaac swipes a drop with his finger and tastes it: sweet, hot copper. More like blood than plastic. Strange. Did Tom's blood taste like this? There's no way of knowing now, but his blood was most likely bitter with booze and antidepressants. As much as Isaac enjoys the sweetness, his goal with the doll is accuracy, not fantasy.

He digs a half-full bottle of Tom's Lexapro out of the nightstand and a fifth of gin from the liquor cabinet in Tom's study—two things he couldn't bear to throw out. Tom wasn't supposed to drink while on his medication, but he lived by his own rules. Isaac places one of the pills in the doll's rubbery mouth, then chases it down with a few glugs of gin. When he shakes the doll, the liquid sloshes into its hollowness. He sits on the bloodstained bed and waits. For what, he's not sure.

His phone's vibration breaks his attention. Just as he looks at the screen—an email about his first, of twelve monthly, payments on the doll—someone burps. Initially, he can't tell if the sound came from himself or the doll. It's only when the pine scent of gin hits him that he knows. He tosses his phone to the floor and holds his hand an inch above the doll's mouth. No breath. At least not yet. Isaac's heart beats double time.

"Can you speak?" he asks. "Say something. Please…"

The doll stays silent.

For a moment, Isaac feels embarrassed. In what reality would a doll come to life? But he knows what he heard and what he smelled. Maybe, just maybe, the doll is more than it seems.

***

Saturday morning. The doll is dressed in Tom's lazy clothes: airy silk pajama bottoms and a peach bathrobe somehow still fluffy after a hundred washes. Isaac places the doll on the balcony overlooking LA's smoggy downtown. Neighbors might double take at the sight, but he doesn't care. This is how Tom spent every Saturday morning: lounging with an iced coffee and a thriller paperback. Death shouldn't stop him from doing what he loves. Yesterday, Isaac picked up P.J. Vernon's *Bath Haus*, which they'd planned to read together along with a pound of Tom's favorite Ethiopian coffee. A thermos of cold brew rests in the doll's right hand and the thriller in its right.

When the scene is perfectly set, Isaac pulls up a second deck chair. He sits down, takes a deep breath, and tries not to look directly at the doll. After all, it held in that burp yesterday until he turned away. Maybe it's shy.

A few minutes pass with nothing but the roar of traffic and wind rustling the palm trees. Then, a new sound: a page turning. Isaac's body buzzes with excitement, but he doesn't dare turn toward the doll. Another page turns. Happy tears well in his eyes. The sound of sipping … followed by spitting. He freezes, then jumps at the *thunk* and *splash* of two objects hitting the balcony's concrete floor. Something tells him the doll wants him to see this, so he turns.

The spilled thermos has landed a good six feet away from the doll. So has the book, now stained brown and dripping with cold brew. As Isaac cleans up the mess, he wonders how well he really knew his husband. He wonders if death changed him.

✳✳✳

Isaac brings the doll to the Indian restaurant where he and Tom had their first date. He knows how this date with a doll will look to the other patrons, so he's reserved a private dining room.

"Come," the wide-eyed owner says with a strained smile. "Quickly now."

Isaac trails the man, grunting as he drags the doll behind him. It's heavier now, its hollow parts filled with sand. When they reach the private dining room, the owner shuts the door the second Isaac steps inside. Isaac seats the doll, then sits on the opposite side on the table. He admires the crisp black tablecloth, the white candle with its soft, comforting flame. A quick glance at the menu tells him it hasn't changed since he and Tom first came here. He smiles, then orders exactly what they ordered twenty years ago.

While waiting for the food, Isaac makes conversation with the doll.

"This must be strange for you," he says, "but I know we can make it work. And it's okay if you've changed, you know? The book, the coffee … none of that matters. What matters is that we're together. That you're here now."

The one-sided conversation continues until the food arrives: silver platters of basmati rice and bright orange tandoori chicken. The owner avoids eye contact as he places the food down, then offers a cursory "enjoy" before rushing out of the room.

Isaac grins at the doll, then looks down at the steaming dish.

"I know you don't like being watched," he says. "And I wish I could look into your eyes right now, but … small sacrifices. You can eat in peace. I promise I won't stare."

He keeps his eyes locked on the plate, asking questions between bites. The food tastes dry and bland, not like it did years ago. Hopefully the change won't interfere with Tom's resurrection. Isaac isn't sure how this magic works, but he senses that recreating memories with accuracy is important. Between bites, he asks questions that go unanswered: "Was there something I could have done to keep you from killing yourself?" "What was it like being dead?" "Are you glad to be back?" "Want to grab a drink after this?"

After this fourth question, Isaac hears the clink of silverware. He stops chewing his dry chicken but resists the urge to look up. The sound continues: a knife slicing meat. Isaac's eyes get hot with tears. It's finally happening. His first date with Tom in six months.

But his gut tightens when the slicing sound continues longer than expected, as if the doll were carving a whole chicken rather than just a leg. He wants to look more than anything, but he chooses to be sneaky, spying with the reflection of his silver plate. He tilts it in the doll's direction until he finds the perfect angle.

That's when he sees it: knife dragging across silicone, cut neck yawning open like a toothless maw, and sand spilling into the doll's lap with a soft *shhhhhh*. Isaac screams and jumps, tipping the table with a crash. Shards of glass and grains of rice spill across the maroon carpet. Isaac lunges at the doll and wrests the knife from its hand, splintering the chair with the force of his landing. Gaping, he cradles the wounded doll, unsure how to save it.

The restaurant owner bursts through the door. Immediately, he puffs out his chest and points to the exit.

"Get out! Just get the hell out!" he screams.

Lifting the doll and pressing a hand to its leaking neck, Isaac flees the restaurant.

***

Isaac is glad he held onto the BDSM gear because he has an even better use for it now. The doll's arms are handcuffed to the bedposts. Its neck still looks ragged, but glue clamps the wound shut. Isaac sits on the bed with a glass of water and a bottle of Lexapro.

"It was my fault," he says. "I shouldn't have let you take your meds with alcohol. They interact poorly and—and I'm sure that's why you acted the way you did tonight. I know you like gin, but just water this time, okay? And I'll double your Lexapro dosage just in case."

Isaac places two pills on the doll's tongue and washes them down with a small pour of water. Before he can pull away, the pills geyser straight into his eye.

Stunned, he blinks but doesn't wipe away the wet.

"You really are alive," he says, trembling. "I don't know how, but I ... I can't lose you, okay? Not again."

He plucks the pills from the bedspread and tries to administer them once more. The doll accepts them without resistance this time, jaw loose and lips parted. Isaac smiles, then slips into bed. Finding a comfortable position is difficult with the doll handcuffed to both sides, but he makes do, curling up like a fetus against its abdomen. Something vibrates against his cheek—the doll either purring or growling. He chooses to believe the former.

***

The doll's hands are severed. It must have worked its wrists back and forth against the handcuffs for hours to slice through the silicone. Isaac's earplugs must have shut the sound out, but what finally wakes him is the handless doll thunking to the floor. The residue of sleep clings to Isaac, and he can't make sense of what he's seeing: a bed full of sand and a loose hand in front of him, waving goodbye or perhaps just seeming to.

When he removes his earplugs, the dragging sound springs him into action. Sitting up, he spies the prone doll inching toward the door. One leap from the mattress and he's on top of it. The doll thrashes underneath him like a pinned crocodile. Sand leaks from its wrists. Emptying out, the doll loses shape and compresses under Isaac's weight. The strength of its thrashing diminishes until it is once more motionless. Isaac rests on top, gasping for air. He scarcely catches his breath before the sobs take over.

"Why'd you do it?" he asks. "I can't move on if I don't know."

For a long moment, his shaky breath is the only sound. The carpet muffles even the faintest white noise. And then the silence breaks. The doll is facedown, but Isaac hears it loud and clear, something that soothes and disturbs him in equal measure: *shhhhhh*.

When the sound dies, an aching, empty quiet settles over the room. An absence both physical and spiritual. It's all over. It's all over.

***

The stink of burning silicone will never leave Isaac's nose. Lighting up the night, the barrel of fire crackles and bubbles, solid becoming liquid becoming pollution. Maybe the city's smog is just a congregation of spirits turned acidic from their time on Earth.

Watching the doll's eyes melt, Isaac resists the impulse to reach into the fire and save the warped, blackened wreckage of his husband. If he tried, there would be little to salvage. And if eyes are the windows to the soul, then Tom's soul is gone, boiled away in a hungry flame. Isaac realizes he'll never know why Tom killed himself. Maybe even Tom didn't know. Isaac could follow him. He could do it tonight with a bottle of sleeping pills. But something quiets that darkest of thoughts, a sound carried on the acrid wind: *shhhhhh*

.

Angel Teeth

(First published by *Starward Shadows Quarterly*)

Celine couldn't believe her brother named his kid after himself. Since when did Mike grow such a big ego? Then again, Celine hadn't seen or talked to him in eighteen months. A lot can change in that much time. But the name thing didn't really matter. What mattered was that Celine—childless now at twenty-one and probably forever, given how things were going—was finally an aunt.

The public library was her go-to place for free internet and fantasy paperbacks, and there she sat on the carpet between the bookshelves, staring at the first Instagram picture of Michael Jr. The boy was pink and wrinkly with a surprisingly long shock of black hair. The caption declared him a seven-pound-three-ounce miracle. A miracle Celine would never see in person if her life didn't do a full one-eighty.

A sob welled up inside her. She covered her mouth to muffle it, not wanting to cause a disruption and get kicked out of the library. The security guard had escorted her off the premises last week for panhandling near the circulation desk, and he'd take any excuse he could get to do it again. Outside, the fierce winter wind blew horizontal sheets of slush. The gusts had nearly whisked away Celine's tent that morning. She'd lined the wet nylon floor with rocks to pin it down, but there was no telling if the tent would still be there when the library closed.

All at once, the narrow space between bookshelves felt claustrophobic. Short of breath, Celine stood up, unzipped her coat, and rushed past the common area toward the restroom. The door didn't have a lock—the library didn't trust people like her behind locked doors—but she made do with what little privacy the restroom afforded. After splashing her face with metallic-smelling sink water, she looked at herself in the cloudy mirror. Dozens of purple scabs adorned her face—"junkie constellations," a homeless shelter volunteer had called them (one of many reasons she'd never gone back to the place). But her teeth were even worse: black around the edges, gray at the roots, and stinking of chemical rot.

She imagined leaning over Michael Jr.'s crib with that grisly smile and being met with terror. His scream would destroy her. Still, she had to see him, and that meant finding a way to hide the damage the past eighteen months had done to her mind, body, and soul.

Her family knew nothing of it. She'd simply slipped out of her parents' house one evening and never returned. They probably figured she'd been murdered or trafficked on the way to her Intermediate Painting night class. The truth still involved shady people but not the type to pull women into vans with tinted windows. No, these people were art school soon-to-be-dropouts selling Oxy to pay tuition. These people were Celine's friends. If Celine did get to see her family again, she'd weave them an explanation of her absence that didn't involve such friends. An explanation that would quell her parents' anger and put their suspicions to rest. With any luck, they'd welcome her back home with open arms. Not that her luck had been holding up as of late.

Celine closed her eyes and listened to the restroom's buzzing fluorescent lights. The electric noise gave her a headache, pain pulsing through her throbbing jaw. Every muscle in her body felt either tight and knotted or loose and useless. She steadied herself on the sink and sobbed, choking and gasping for breath. It was obvious what she needed to feel right again. Hopefully her last fifteen bucks would be enough to get it.

She checked the weather app on her phone; a cold front was coming. The slush outside would freeze soon. And even though the library was still open for another four hours, Celine ran out into the cold, off to see her dealer.

***

Doug didn't like when Celine came in through the car shop's front entrance, so Celine shot him a text and waited out back. The ice had downed a power line running through the alley, and the wind had built to a piercing gale. Small, sharp snow crystals stung Celine's face. Her thin cotton gloves did little to keep her fingers from purpling.

"Fuck, fuck, fuck," she said. "C'mon, Doug."

The one good thing about standing out in a blizzard was that she could more easily ignore her withdrawal symptoms. The cold numbed her headache and lessened her fever, or at least seemed to. And full-body shivers distracted from her nausea. Her coat leaked puffs of insulation from a dozen different holes, making it easy for body heat to escape. Her camp was two miles away, far enough that the first signs of frostbite would creep gray into her fingers by the time she got there on foot. If Doug made her wait any longer, she'd have to enter the car shop through the front door. What did it matter if he got pissed? He'd tolerate the transgression so long as Celine remained a loyal customer.

That was when Doug opened the back door. He squinted at the blowing snow, his brown mustache twitching in displeasure. He wore a blue mechanic's jumpsuit stained with many years of grease. A patch on the breast read "William," the name he used for his more legitimate business dealings. He gestured for Celine to follow him inside. She practically ran after him, stepping on his boot heels as they walked to the break room together.

"You look cold, Celly," Doug said, flopping down on the black leather couch. He removed his gloves and tossed them into the concrete corner.

"Yeah, I had to wait outside," Celine said. She hoped her tone wouldn't drive up Doug's ever-fluctuating prices. It was a mystery how the man decided what a hit would cost on any given day.

"What do you think would happen to me—or you, for that matter—if a bunch of scarred-up junkies lined up outside my shop?"

Celine waved her hand as if to say *I know* and excuse her pissiness. "What can fifteen get me?"

Doug slumped his head and laughed. "You're kidding me, right? Nothing. It gets you nothing. But listen, the new guy I hired part-time is useless. Didn't show up today. You know how to replace a transmission? You do that for me and I'll give you enough to keep you high for a couple days."

Celine didn't realize she was crying until Doug's eyes softened. He scooted to the far side of the couch and patted the cushion beside him. Celine sat down. Her legs felt like jelly. She imagined how nice it would be to take a nap back there in the relative warmth, the hum of Doug's minifridge soothing her to sleep while clipped-out *Sports Illustrated* swimsuit models watched over her from one wall and pictures of Doug's mother watched over her from the other.

"Maybe that's for the best," she said, scratching at her arm's dry skin. "I need to quit. For my nephew."

"Never heard you mention a nephew before," Doug said, eying the wall clock.

"Born today. I … I want to be clean before I see him."

Doug stared at the wall, sniffed once, and tapped his temple with a greasy finger.

"Here, I'll show you a picture of him," Celine continued, grasping for her phone with her still-stiff fingers. "He's adorable. I— I think you'll understand why I need to—"

"Listen," Doug said, waving away the phone. "Got something that might help you with that. How much money did you say you had on you? Fifteen bucks?"

"Yeah."

"Well, consider that a down payment. You can pay the rest when you get clean and get a job. And trust me, this thing'll get you clean. I … hmm…"

Doug's gaze drifted to the floor. He blinked quickly as if weighing a decision. Celine put a hand on his shoulder, but Doug pulled away.

"Don't," he said. "I hate when people—"

"Sorry, sorry," Celine replied. "But what is it? Please."

"Okay, I'll show you, but you can't tell a fuckin' soul. And … and you should know that it's a powerful solution but not a perfect one."

"Sure, yeah, what is it?"

Doug took a deep breath and puffed out his cheeks for the exhale. He clapped both hands on his thighs, then got up.

"Follow me," he said. "And for the love of God, don't scream when you see it."

***

The office door had three separate locks: deadbolt, padlock, and keypad. Given that Doug stored his drugs in a different room with only two locks, Celine had to wonder what was inside this one. Maybe there was a safe full of cash, or maybe Doug trafficked in goods even worse than the ones he sold Celine.

While waiting for him to unlock the door, Celine's body warmed under the whirring garage heater. Her withdrawal symptoms returned as she thawed out. A throbbing pain pounded a steady rhythm between her eyes and a tremor coursed through both hands. Doug finally got the door open but blocked the way with his body.

"Like I said, be chill, okay?" he said.

Celine nodded, then frowned. The oily musk pervading the garage had vanished. The smell of honeysuckle and spring rain wafted out of the mystery room. It smelled too much like the real thing to come from a plug-in air freshener. The aroma brought

Celine back to her childhood wandering her family's flower garden, listening to the soft patter of rain against her jacket, and watching her father tend to the tulips. She felt the peace of that memory as if it were happening once more. Her eyes watered.

"You coming?" Doug snapped.

Celine shook herself out of it and followed him into the room. Doug bolted the door shut as soon as she was inside. It was then that Celine understood why he'd warned her not to scream.

It—whatever it was—stood tall enough that its head scraped the ceiling. Chains held its pale wrists and ankles, which leaked a fluid that looked like the oozing guts of a star. *Blood?* Two massive wings hung from the creature's back, white feathers scorched black at their ends. Its solid gold eyes bulged out like an insect's. Holding its gaze for more than a few seconds made Celine's heart pound as if it might explode, so she looked away.

"What is it?" Her voice shuddered.

"What's it look like? It's an angel, Celly."

"I didn't think that—"

Doug laughed nervously and picked up a Rubik's cube from his desk. He twirled it in his hand for a few seconds before setting it down again.

Celine stared at the angel through her peripherals, afraid to look at it head-on; the creature took up more than half of the room.

"Where did it come from? How'd you get it here?" she asked, wincing as the angel groaned against its chains, vocal tones layered like a dissonant choir.

"You don't want to know," Doug said. "But listen, this thing is a literal miracle worker. My mom—bless her heart, I love the woman —has leukemia. Excuse me, *had* leukemia. Cleared up a few days after I injected her with angel blood. *Purity rooting out corruption.* That's what the book said. Anyway, Mom is doing great, uh, minus a few side—"

"Can it cure me?" Celine got close enough to Doug that she could feel his heat.

"Damn right it can," he said, taking a big step back. "But like I was trying to say, there are side effects."

"Meth has side effects, too. But you've been selling that to me for—"

"Yeah, yeah, yeah. But the angel's side effects are …" Drops of sweat trailed down Doug's forehead. He wiped them off and turned away from the angel. "Ah, fuck it. You're not going to care either way, are you?"

Celine shook her head.

Doug sighed. "Well, let's get this over with. Show me your teeth."

Celine hesitated, then tugged down her lower lip to show the ruin of crumbling enamel and gums pocked with gray sores. Doug winced, then rummaged through a desk drawer until he found a pair of pliers. He turned toward the angel, which thrashed in its chain as if anticipating what was to come.

"Right, Celly," Doug said. "Let's get you some new pearly whites."

***

The angel screamed like a Nazgûl. Celine was sure a customer outside would hear. Or worse yet, the angel's brethren. She imagined a celestial army converging on the car shop, armed with flaming swords and God's ceaseless wrath.

Doug wore ear protection as he stood atop the squeaky folding chair and ripped out the angel's teeth with pliers. Tangerine blood sprayed his jumpsuit, but he didn't pay it any mind—just pocketed each tooth like a lucky penny and kept working.

A sweet floral aroma emanated from the angel's wounds. The smell calmed Celine, but it wasn't enough to fully suppress her terror. Pressed into the corner of the room, she watched the carnage with unblinking eyes. She imagined the angel escaping its chains and tearing the office apart, splattering every wall with the viscera of sinners. But the creature's thrashing diminished with each tooth Doug extracted. When its Nazgûl howls became harmonic whimpers, Celine's fear faded into a vague pity. An ulcerous pain settled in her gut.

Doug removed the final tooth and stepped down from the chair. He grabbed a greasy towel from his back pocket and wiped sweat and blood from his face. His breaths were ragged.

"Like I said, the fifteen bucks is just a down payment. I don't do this shit for under a thousand."

"A thousand?" Celine balled her hands into fists.

"It's a lot easier to save that much when you're clean, and it's a lot easier to get clean when you've got angel teeth. You want these things or not?"

"Do you … have to take mine out, too?"

A visible shudder ran through Doug. It was harder to rip teeth out of a human being—and friendly acquaintance, no less—than something as monstrous as the creature behind him.

"You want to be part of your nephew's life, right?" he asked.

Celine's eyes welled with tears. She breathed deep, readied herself for lightning-hot agony, then nodded.

"That's what I figured," Doug said. "Now open your mouth."

***

By the fifth molar, Celine wished she'd stayed out in the blizzard and let her fingers, toes, and face blacken with frostbite. At least then she would've been numb to all pain.

But the torture didn't last long—Doug worked as if he were trying to beat a Guinness World Record—and what followed was the antithesis of pain. When Doug slid the first angel tooth into place, it doused the fire that scorched every nerve in Celine's body. A tingly, floaty sensation replaced the burn and caressed her gums. Celine wondered if Doug had slipped her some fast-acting opiate, but no, he'd only inserted the tooth, which slithered into place and rooted itself as if it had a mind of its own. With each one that followed, the sensation mounted into something more transcendent than Celine had felt on any drug. Joyful tears ran down her cheeks. Residual fear vanished like smoke carried off on a honeyed wind.

Doug placed the final tooth as if it were the topper for a wedding cake. Puffing out his cheeks, he stepped back to admire his handiwork. He grinned, then covered his mouth.

"Shit, your pearlies look better than mine now," he said. "I could use some whitening strips. Let's get you to the bathroom. You can clean the blood off your face and take a look in the mirror."

Bathed in a haze of endorphins, Celine smiled and followed Doug out of the office. She gazed at the slumped angel on her way out. All at once, the reality of what she'd done threatened to evaporate her high.

"Don't," Doug said, shutting the door and triple-locking it. "It's best not to look back. Trust me."

Celine closed her eyes and did what she'd done many times in art school to steer herself clear of a bad trip. Light danced behind her eyes. Effervescence coursed through her veins and tickled her pleasantly from the inside. The angel faded from memory, at least for the moment.

Doug led her to the bathroom. In the mirror, Celine examined herself: neck drenched in blood, chin clumpy with purple clots. But her teeth—oh, her teeth! Toothpaste commercial white and immaculately straight.

"They look beautiful," Celine said, jostling one of her new incisors. It held firm.

"And I don't even have a dentistry license," Doug said. "Changes your whole face, doesn't it?"

Something else had changed, too. Celine leaned closer to the greasy mirror.

"My scabs," she said, scratching one of them. It came off as a dry red flake. The skin underneath was soft and smooth with no signs of scarring.

"Please, God, don't pick that shit off yourself while you're in here," Doug said, shaking his head.

"Sorry, I'm just—it seems too good to be true. I don't need to come back for more … treatments?"

"Yeah, no, it's amazing. One and done. Listen, I'll be calling you next month. We can space out the payments, but I want two hundred bucks by the first, okay?"

Celine grinned at Doug in the mirror: "I know you hate when people touch you, but I'd love to give you a hug right now. I'll have your money."

"Good, good," Doug said, turning as if to leave and then stopping. "And uh, have fun with your nephew."

Celine beamed, her new smile stretching so wide that it felt like her face would break. It was time to pick off the rest of these scabs in the alleyway and then call her brother for a ride.

***

The car ride into the suburbs was dead silent. Celine alternated between smiling to herself and then remembering how she'd gotten that smile. It was hard to suppress joy for long though. Her withdrawal symptoms had vanished. There was no longer that demon inside her screaming for its next fix. The teeth had made sure of that. *The angel …*

Celine must have looked insane with her ever-vacillating expressions. Mike glanced over at her every other minute, eyebrow raised and mouth curled, but refused to speak. The silence could only last so long though. It ended when they reached a particularly long red light.

Snow came down in thick flakes, carpeting the pavement and slowing traffic in all directions. The van ahead had its emergency lights on, stuck on the incline and going nowhere fast. Mike sighed, tapped the steering wheel as if it might speed up time, and finally turned to Celine.

"I just don't understand," he said. "All this time … two years."

"Eighteen months," Celine corrected.

"Whatever. Too damn long."

Celine's eyes widened. Mike never swore. Or, if he did, it was a habit he'd picked up in the time she'd been away. Sadness consumed her as she thought of all she'd missed: going bowling with Mike each Sunday after church, painting along with her mother during Bob Ross reruns, and arguing politics with her father any chance she got. She even missed the not-so-great parts: the church's shitty live "rock" band, her mother's criticisms of her painting technique, and her father's tendency to give her the silent treatment after they argued.

"You were gone all that time and never thought to tell us what was happening," Mike asked. "Where were you anyway?"

Celine had rehearsed an answer countless times. A dozen believable stories were fleshed out and ready to be performed, but suddenly she couldn't access any of them. Or at least couldn't translate them into words. The strangeness of this day had scrambled her.

"I'll wait until we get to Mom and Dad's," she said. "I'd prefer not to explain it twice. Will Michael Jr. be there?"

Mike squinted as if assessing how Celine knew about the baby. But he shook his head in lieu of responding to her question.

"Assuming we don't get stuck in the snow, we'll be there in five minutes," he said. "Better polish up your lie."

Celine's face flushed with heat. She turned toward the window and pretended to watch the snow.

***

Celine's mother cried and screamed. Her father sulked and tried to hide his wet eyes. Mike tuned everything out and texted frantically on his phone. It wasn't the worst possible homecoming, but it was far from the best.

"Do you know how worried we've been?" Celine's mother asked, voice leaping wildly between pitches. "We filed police reports, we hired a private investigator, we prayed every—"

"Janice, stop it," Celine's father said, grabbing a beer from the fridge.

Celine hoped her father would defend her from the barrage of questions, but that hope was short-lived.

The man sat on the couch, cracked open his beer can, and continued: "Celine will give us the full story when she feels comfortable."

His eyes were a cold, piercing blue. The eyes of a cop in an interrogation.

Celine averted her gaze and looked at the Christmas tree at the center of her parents' living room. Plenty of gifts sat below the tree, but none with her name on them. Had they assumed she was dead after all this time? The thought was too painful, so Celine looked to the top of the tree where the angel ornament rested. It looked nothing like Doug's angel—the angel she'd tormented, but the memory of its screeching agony flashed in her mind. She blinked to clear it away. When she opened her eyes, the angel ornament twitched. Celine jumped.

"What's wrong, Celine?" her father asked, half-standing.

Hand over her heart, Celine noticed the family cat Merv brushing his face against the tree. The angel ornament hadn't moved on its own. Of course it hadn't.

"Nothing," Celine said. "I'm fine. Sorry."

"Listen, Celine. Your clothes look and, frankly, *smell* like they've seen better days," her father said. "Why don't you wash up and change into some fresh ones from your old room—if you remember where that is—and then come talk to us?"

Celine blushed as she examined her sour jeans and stained sweater. It had been weeks since her last trip to the laundromat. In the financial battle between clean underwear and her next hit, the latter had almost always won. To think that now dry socks sounded nicer than a cloud of meth swirling around her lungs. It was strange and wonderful, courtesy of a mutilated angel.

"I'll get changed," Celine said. "But I want to see Michael Jr. when I get back. Angie's bringing him over, right?"

Mike opened his mouth to respond, then closed it and swallowed hard. He nodded. Sweat slicked his brow.

Celine was a stranger in her old home. She excused herself to change into the clothes of someone more familiar.

***

Her room hadn't changed since she'd last been inside it eighteen months ago. Back then, she'd been living at home and taking studio art classes. She'd wanted an apartment of her own, but college was expensive. Her parents' nagging was the price she'd paid for free room and board. *Celine, why don't you choose another major? Celine, when are you going to get a job? Celine, what are you even doing with your life? Celine, Celine, Celine …*

Wrapped in a fresh bathrobe, Celine scanned the room. There was dust atop the dresser, a crusty dish on the nightstand. Her mother had always been insistent that Celine clean up after herself, so it didn't surprise Celine that the dish—certainly her own—was still there. She smiled and shook her head. But something about the room saddened her. The air smelled musty, ancient, tomblike. The residence of a woman now dead. Assuming her parents let her stay for a while, she'd spruce up her bedroom and take better care of it than she ever had before. Her mother would poke her head in but find no mess to complain about. They'd exchange a smile: her mother's brittle and adorned with crowns, and Celine's perfectly angelic.

Still, there was no guarantee Celine would be welcome back. If she told them the truth about her absence, they'd forever see her as a lowlife. But if she invented a more glamorous story, they'd know she was lying; her father was practically a human polygraph machine. The third option was "don't ask, don't tell." This approach was quintessentially Midwestern: a theatre of buried secrets, heavy silences, and polite restraint. But it didn't feel right. No option did.

Celine was crying again. How many times had that happened today? She wiped her cheeks, sniffled, and then walked to the dresser. Before she could grip the dusty handle and open the drawer, the backyard motion sensor light activated, shining through the sheer curtains. Her parents and brother were whispering to each other in the living room. Maybe Angie and Michael Jr. were coming in through the back door.

That notion evaporated as soon as a shadow passed across the window. The figure was too tall to be Angie. Too tall to be human at all. Its head extended far above the top of the window. It paced back and forth, lurching but soundless. Celine only saw it in profile until it stopped for a long moment, then turned to face her. She gasped as it revealed the sprawling silhouette of wings. The feathers ruffled violently, not by some incidental gust of wind but by the seething of flesh beneath.

Celine concealed a scream and bolted. When she entered the living room, trembling and tense, her father raised an eyebrow.

"You didn't change clothes, Celine. I told you, your old ones are —"

"They don't fit," Celine said, her words spilling out too fast. She took a breath and slowed down her speech. "I … I lost some weight. They're all too big."

Her father squinted, looking her up and down. His eyes lingered on her teeth.

"Yeah, you do look different," he said, not in a way that agreed with her story but rather, invited more questions.

The front door clicked open. Celine ran backward, an involuntary flight response, and tripped over the wooden coffee table. Her ribs smashed into the table's corner. She let out a yelp, clutching the wound and writhing on the floor.

"Celine, why the hell are you so jumpy tonight? Get up," her father asked, setting down a second beer can and bending down to help her up.

Pain fading, Celine looked up to see Angie entering the house, snow dusting her shoulders and a blanketed bundle in her arms. Angie beamed and rushed over to greet Celine.

"God, I've missed you so much," she said, hugging Celine with her free arm. The woman's eyes glistened with happy tears.

Angie's words soothed the pain in Celine's side. The woman had always been so sincere in her kindness. It felt good to know at least one person was happy to have her back.

"This is Michael Jr.," Angie said.

Celine looked at Angie's bundle. It was him. She couldn't believe it. Her nephew was real.

***

Celine held Michael Jr. for a long time. He was still the Pepto Bismal pink of an infant, but his eyes were open now—deep brown with a starlight sparkle. Celine rocked him gently and held his gaze. His gummy smile melted her heart and filled her eyes with tears. Peace. Pure peace. Celine's body didn't cry out for poison. Her mind didn't stray to the monstrous silhouette she'd seen from her old bedroom. She wanted to stay in this moment forever—just her and this beautiful boy.

Mike sat beside Angie on the couch, whispering to her with a hand cupped over his mouth. Celine's mother sat on the recliner with eyes closed, mouthing a silent prayer. Celine's father prepared a pot of coffee for the long night ahead. The air felt thick with anticipation, like a soldier's finger on the trigger. Its heaviness threatened to puncture Celine's moment of serenity, but she could endure it as long as Michael Jr. was in her arms.

It was the window above the TV rattling that ripped Celine fully out of the moment. No one else paid the sound any mind, but it grew louder and more violent as if the glass might burst any second. The knowledge that it was blizzarding outside did nothing to halt Celine's paranoia. What if it wasn't the wind shaking the glass? What if that angel really had escaped and come to hunt her down? How well could a quarter-inch of glass protect her? For once, she hoped she was having an hallucination.

The stench of a freshly-filled diaper brought her back to reality. "He needs a change," she said, standing up with Michael Jr. in her shaky arms.

Mike leaned forward as if to pop up and stop her, but he eased back into his seat when Angie grabbed his arm. Mike's eyes followed as Celine walked to the bathroom.

Despite the bathroom's smallness and Michael Jr.'s pungency, Celine found it easier to breathe with the door closed. Everything felt better when it was just her and Michael Jr. in a windowless room, free from the gaze of angels hungry for blood and family members hungry for terrible, terrible answers.

She set a towel on the floor and rested him atop it, then searched the cabinet for diapers. After finding a fresh one, she unbundled the boy from his pale yellow blanket and removed the diaper he'd soiled.

It was only when she lifted his butt that she noticed the feathers. Downy clusters across his upper back: white, soft, and tiny. She hoped they'd come from the blanket's stuffing, but her gut twisted at the other possibility. She hesitated before plucking at one of the feathers. It didn't peel away from Michael Jr.'s sticky flesh; the quill was firmly embedded inside him. The skin around it whitened when Celine pulled.

Again, she wouldn't scream. She refused to. Her family would interpret her terror as a sign of mental instability. A sign that she posed a threat to Michael Jr. They'd seen her jump at the sight of a swaying Christmas ornament and flee at the sound of an opening door. Two strikes against her already. She wouldn't earn a third. No, she'd finish changing the diaper, go back out there, and face her family, calm and collected.

The diaper change was lightning fast and far from perfect. She fastened the diaper too loosely, but it would have to do. She wrapped the blanket tightly around Michael Jr. next. No feathers poked out from the bundle, but even with them hidden, she couldn't pretend they weren't there. The universe had given her plenty of signs tonight. She could no longer ignore them.

She took a deep breath, put the bathroom in order, and carried Michael Jr. back into the living room. Her father was pouring cups of coffee for everyone. Somberness choked the room.

"All fresh and clean," Celine said. With shaky arms, she handed Michael Jr. to Angie who smiled and mouthed a *thank you.*

"Sit down," Celine's father said. "Have some coffee."

He thrust a cup into her hands, a few drops spilling over the rim. Celine sat in the armchair farthest from the still-rattling window. Her body trembled even worse than it had earlier while waiting in the cold outside the car shop. She steadied her hand and raised the cup to her lips. Everyone watched as she sipped. The coffee scorched her throat and filled her chest with heat. Sweat beaded to the surface of her neck like a suffocating scarf. Every pore on her body burned. How wonderful it would've been to strip naked and flee into the night, to cool the overheated engine that was her body in pure animal distress. But there was no more avoiding it now. The Christmas tree angel gazed down at her with eyes that judged and loved and loathed and commanded. Celine had to tell the truth, even if it meant this would be her first and last time seeing Michael Jr.

"So," she said. Everyone leaned in. "I should probably tell you where I've been …"

***

The world was calm again. No howling wind to deafen nor blowing drifts to blind. Outside the car shop, a blanket of virgin snow sparkled in the rising sun. Customers seeking oil changes would drive up soon and muddy the white, but for now the snow was perfect. Celine stood at the front door, breathing crisp morning air and grazing her foot across a fluffy snowdrift. She carved gentle swirling patterns into the surface, determined to enhance the beauty rather than spoil it.

Her father had given her a ride and parked across the street, his engine still running for heat. He watched her every move. She'd told him she wanted to apply for a job here, which wasn't entirely untrue. Doug worked himself to the bone and would likely welcome extra help from someone who wouldn't rat to the cops about his side hustle. Celine couldn't replace a brake pad or even a headlight, but she could learn. However, she had another motive for coming here, too. Something far more important.

Doug pulled into the lot a little before seven in the morning. When he saw Celine out front, he rubbed his eyes with his thumb and forefinger, then lumbered in her direction.

"What's up, Celly?" he asked. "Actually, don't answer that. We'll talk inside. Has to be quick though. Some guy's dropping off his beater in ten."

Before following Doug inside, Celine looked to her dad in his truck and smiled. His expression was stern as ever, but he raised his coffee thermos and nodded at her. Celine turned away and entered the car shop.

"So, what is it, Celly?" Doug said, pulling on some work gloves. "You already got the thousand bucks for me or what? No other reason for you to be here given that you're clean and cured."

"Actually," Celine said. "I was hoping I could apply for a job."

Doug did a double take. After a pause, he walked behind the cash register and silently counted the drawer.

"You don't know anything about cars," he said after finishing with a stack of tens.

"Okay, then don't hire me."

Doug glanced up, smirked, and set down the stack of fives he'd just picked up.

"It's too early for games, Celly. What the hell do you want?"

"I want to see the angel again."

Doug's smirk faded. His tense shoulders seemed to deflate. He cleared his throat as if something more than just phlegm were blocking it. Whatever count he'd had on the drawer was forgotten. He shoved the stack back in the cash drawer before slamming it shut, then flicked through his keyring until he found what he needed.

"You and me both," he said, and for once, his voice sounded tender, haunted. "I … I've been trying, you know? Not sure what I have to do to … anyway, maybe you'll have better luck. Let's go."

***

Somehow the angel clung to life. Gallons of yesterday's blood had congealed on the floor, the color and consistency of honey. Its sweetness was more floral than sickly. The creature barely lifted its head when Celine and Doug entered the room. Maybe it could sense their intentions and knew they didn't plan to torture it further.

Celine approached without hesitation and looked the angel in its golden eyes. Her knees trembled and her stomach boiled, but she refused to flee. Her life could not go on if she did. She reached out for Doug's hand behind her. This time he didn't recoil at her touch. His hand was cold and calloused, but it gave her comfort. She hoped her hand did the same for him.

"Angel," she said, and the word sounded silly coming from her mouth. The creature probably had a name and a thousand years of deeds behind it. But Celine was doing her best with what little information she had.

"I've done horrible things to you," she continued. "Unforgivable things. And yet here I am begging you for forgiveness. Because of you, I have a future again. I have my health. I have my family. My nephew."

Celine drew in a shuddering breath. Doug squeezed her hand, his touch no longer cold.

"I can't enjoy all you've given me unless you forgive what I've taken," Celine said. "But I know it's stupid and selfish to ask. If you aren't willing to do it, I … I'll give back your teeth. I'll…"

The angel raised its head so abruptly that its thick chains rattled. Celine backed into Doug. He gripped her shoulders and seemed ready to pull her out of the room at the first sign of danger. The angel leaned forward as far as its restraints allowed, then opened its cavernous mouth. Inside was the white-barbed flesh of its tongue and the craters of vacant gums, jellied with orange gore. Celine backed up a step further, convinced the creature would bite her, but then she saw it: the crowns of new teeth rising into place, populating the angel's mouth with fresh ivory. The teeth rose fully into place, then popped loose all at once and pittered to the syrupy floor. Another set rose swiftly behind them, then tumbled out just the same. The cycle repeated again and again, and each time, Celine wanted to back further away but found herself too entranced to do so. Finally, with hundreds of teeth littering the floor like shards of milky glass, one last set rose … and stayed in place. The angel smiled. Then it clenched its fists and broke its chains as if they were made of paper. It exhaled a heavy breath that seemed to boil the air. Sweating, Doug staggered backward, but Celine stayed in place as the breath lifted her hair. It smelled of lilacs on a summer night.

The angel's weakness had all been theatre, but Celine's fear vanished regardless. She knew she'd been forgiven. All she'd had to do was ask.

Transubstantiation

(First published by *Dread Stone Press*)

Every week, Father George asks me to confess my sins, and every time I tell him I have none to confess. He always waits a few seconds after that, like he doesn't believe me. It's because the other kids are so bad that he expects me to be that way, too. I won't tell him that though. That would be back-talking, and back-talking is a sin.

"You haven't lied to your mother or father?" he asked me in confession last week.

"No," I said, and I was almost crying. Not because I was guilty but because I didn't want him to think I'm bad. "I never lie to anyone."

"Not even a tiny fib?" he asked.

Then, I really did start crying, but I was behind the confessional screen, so he couldn't see my tears. Mom says that sometimes when people cry, it's because they did a bad thing, an I didn't want Father George to think that was why I was crying. I've been trying my best to stay sinless for the Transubstantiation. That word is hard to pronounce, but I've seen it written enough times that I can spell it out. Sister Mary tested all the third graders on the word's spelling, and I was the only one who got it right. I'm not being prideful, Jesus. I'm just telling the truth.

"Who here knows how it feels to be pure, children?" Sister Mary asked in religion class the other day.

Sitting in the desk beside me, Alan nodded. Sister Mary rushed over and smacked his knuckles with a ruler. He got all red in the face and sucked his fingers.

"None of you," Sister Mary said, "not a single one of you is pure. If any of you prove me wrong on the day of Transubstantiation, you will feel God's eternal light blossom inside you like a flower."

I think she's right—about the other kids, not me. They aren't ready for what's coming. Jacob used the Lord's name in vain when the desk lid fell on his finger. Helen cheated on the math test by writing times tables on her arm. And Matthew lied to his parents about finishing his homework so he could spend the night at my house. Mommy doesn't let him come over anymore.

***

The Transubstantiation is today, and all of the third graders are standing in a single-file line. I'm in the back, which makes me nervous, because the longer I have to wait, the more time I have to sin.

We walk up to the altar one at a time. Father George stands behind a table decorated with candles and a white lace tablecloth. He's holding a plate of bread and a silver cup of wine. The room is dark back where I am, but it gets brighter the closer I get to the candles. A statue of Jesus on the cross hangs from the high ceiling. I've looked at it a hundred times, and today, Jesus seems to look back at me. I can't tell if he's in pain because he's been crucified or because he thinks I've sinned. I almost cry, but I hold the tears in. Daddy says only girls cry, and I'm not a girl.

Father George is speaking now, and I pay attention because you're supposed to do that when an adult talks, unless that adult is an atheist.

"The sinners may consume Christ, but they will not feel His presence," he says, placing the bread on Matthew's lying tongue. "His second coming gestates only inside the pure."

The line moves forward. Kids who have already taken the bread and wine sit in the front pew. They whisper to each other and laugh. I don't understand how they can be so happy when it's obvious that Jesus hasn't chosen them as His vessel. Like Father George said, you'll know it the moment you swallow the sacrament.

I look up at Jesus' statue again, but I'm so close to the altar that I can't see if His face is happy or angry. I crane my head so high up that I don't notice it's my turn until Father George calls me, not once, but twice. I hope he doesn't think I was ignoring him because that would make me a sinner.

I walk forward. Father George hands me the bread.

"Take and eat," he says.

I do. My throat is dry, so I almost choke when I try to swallow. But Father George passes the cup to me. I hold it to my lips, say a silent prayer, and drink. The red wine is bitter and makes me shiver, but I feel an immediate change as soon as I swallow.

BUH-buh, BUH-buh. Like an extra heart beating inside me. It's strong, and it hurts my stomach each time it moves. I look down at my white button-up shirt and see a shape pushing out from my belly button. It reminds me of when Mommy was pregnant with Elise, and Elise kicked her from the inside. I always thought it looked funny, but now that it's happening to me, it's painful. Maybe that's because mommies are made for having babies and boys are not.

Father George sets the cup down and kneels next to me.

"No, it couldn't be," he says, and his eyes are wide and shiny when he looks at the kicking thing under my shirt. "Michael, you were telling the truth when—"

But he can't say anything else because I stumble backwards and fall on the floor and start screaming. There's a sound like cutting through a really tough steak, and I feel my belly ripping. There's a red line on my shirt now. Father George runs over to me and puts a hand on my rip. His mouth is moving really fast, but I shift my head so I can see the Jesus statue behind him. His face is visible again. He's bleeding under the crown of thorns, but he's smiling, too. Smiling at me. And I think I'm still screaming, and I think Father George is screaming too, but I'm smiling right along with Jesus. If He can smile through the pain, then so can I.

There's a wet sound as my rip gets bigger, and now Father George has splotches of blood and chunks of pink on his face. My vision is blurry, but I'm pretty sure he's running away.

Someone's crawling out of me. A big shape, bigger than Father George. So big its head touches the cross hanging high above. And everything's going gray, but I know it's Jesus. I smile even wider, and I do cry now, but it's happy tears, not girl tears. Happy because I remained sinless. Happy because I was blessed to be His vessel.

In His Youth

The following is an excerpt from the journal of Will Holzer, quarterback of the Green Bay Packers. He has been missing for the past six months and is wanted for questioning.

The Journal of Will Holzer

February 12th, 2022

This journal is my own—hidden in the closet beneath my old college jersey—but not all its words belong to me. I recognize my voice in most entries, but others feel completely alien. Even the handwriting looks different: block lettering rather than my typical chicken scratch. It scares me that I've seen that block lettering more often lately.

For the moment, however, my handwriting is as shitty as it should be. And while it's still shitty and I'm still *me*, I've decided to record the events that led to this nightmare. In case I'm not around after tomorrow, I'm leaving this journal on my bed where you can find it, Mom. You're the only one with a spare, and the only one who checks in anymore. I hope this journal explains some things for you. I'm just worried you won't believe me.

This started ten years ago when I was a high school senior. YOU KNOW, THE YEAR MY FOOTBALL TEAM BEAT THE EVENSON HIGH NUMBER ONE RANKED TEAM UNDER THE GREAT LEADERSHIP OF

(I'm sorry. It's happening again).

You were working doubles at the Red Lobster to make up for what Dad refused to pay in child support. Somehow you squirreled away a couple thousand bucks for my college fund, but I still needed a football scholarship to cover the full four years. Now I think my life would have been infinitely better had I blown off college and football entirely. That probably sounds ridiculous to you, what, with me playing for the Packers and living in a lake house. But you'll understand where I'm coming from soon.

Back to senior year. My football team was nearing the end of its season: five wins, four losses. FOUR ON ACCOUNT OF THE OPPOSING TEAMS' WIDESPREAD USE OF PERFORMANCE-ENHANCING DRUGS, I'M SURE OF IT.

(Goddamnit, just let me speak.)

Our record wasn't spectacular, but a fantastic player on a middling team can still go places. I intended to be that player: four years playing college ball, a lengthy NFL career after that, and then a degree in accounting to take care of me when my body could no longer play. I had my whole life planned out. AND WHAT A SPECTACULAR LIFE IT'S BEEN: TWO YEARS AS AN NFL QUARTERBACK, TWO SUPER BOWL CHAMPIONSHIPS, SPONSORSHIP DEALS WITH NIKE, GATORADE, AND

(shut up shut up shut up)

The night before my high school team's final game, I told Coach Warner about these post-high school ambitions. I figured his advice would help. After all, the man won the Heisman Trophy as a college player and had been poised for greatness in the NFL. Unfortunately, a severe head injury cut his career short just half a season in. He spent time in and out of rehabilitation for opioid addiction—LIES—before landing a coaching job at Jefferson High. The fact that the school hired him with full knowledge of his drug issues was a testament to his status in the world of football, A STATUS THAT WILL FOREVER BE CEMENTED IN HISTORY AFTER MY THIRD SUPER BOWL WIN TOMORROW.

(Ignore that, Mom. I promise this will make sense soon.)

Coach Warner agreed to help me on the condition that I never questioned his guidance, even when it sounded strange. I should have seen that as a red flag. After all, we were alone in the weight room and still he chose to whisper, as if his words contained some taboo secret. And I know what you're assuming, Mom, but no, he never touched me. He was a different kind of creep.

Coach and I talked long after sundown. He asked me a thousand questions about my dreams and what I was willing to do to make them happen.

Looking back on those questions now, I think they were more about assessing my obedience than understanding my goals. *Do you trust me completely, Will? Would you ever question your coach's expertise? How much are you willing to sacrifice?*

AND YOU'VE PLAYED YOUR PART WELL. DON'T FUCK IT UP NOW, SON. DON'T DO WHAT I THINK YOU'RE ABOUT TO DO.

Sorry, Mom. I'm shaking. I'll write more when he calms down.

***

I'll never forget the final game of my high school football career. Because of your work schedule, it was the only game you could attend that season. I happy-cried when I saw you in the stands smiling and holding a paper-bag sign with my jersey number Sharpied onto it. Any other player would have been embarrassed if his mom showed up like that, but not me.

Coach Warner had something planned for me that night. He wouldn't tell me what, but he'd spent much of our long conversation hammering home the importance of trust. As long as I kept faith, everything would turn out fine: the game would go beautifully, a recruiter would see my impressive performance, and a good college would offer me a scholarship.

I played well throughout the night, running a few first downs, but I didn't think those would be enough to impress a recruiter. I waited for Coach to give me some guidance, my patience wearing thin as the clock ticked away any chance to prove myself.

In the fourth quarter, our team was down by three points with ten seconds on the clock. Coach called a timeout, and we huddled around him. What he said surprised everyone.

"Gentlemen, I want you to keep an eye on Will. He's about to do great things. Now get back out there!"

No one moved. The other guys stared at me with blank, sweaty expressions. All I could do was shrug, just as confused as they were. Then, Coach slapped my shoulder pad, pushed me toward the field. Everyone followed as if I were a train engine and they were the cars in tow. Before the clock started again, I glanced back. Coach sat on the shadowed edge of the floodlights, breath rolling out in thick white puffs before dissipating into the November night. His eyes were closed as if in prayer. It seemed the man didn't have a plan for me, instead counting on God to intervene on my behalf. It had been years since you had last forced me to attend church, so I doubted God would step in now.

But I wasn't entirely convinced Coach was praying. There was the scarier possibility that his head trauma was to blame for this momentary break from reality. The team saw the effects of this trauma any time he forgot our names, lay down on the field with an incapacitating migraine, or zoned out in the middle of team dinners at the pizza buffet. None of those moments lessened our faith in Coach, but this bizarre ten-seconds-on-the-clock huddle visibly shook us. EVEN NOW, AFTER ALL OF YOUR BODY'S VICTORIES, YOU DOUBT ME. I AM YOUR GUIDE. I AM YOUR SAVIOR. WITHOUT ME, YOU ARE

(stop stop stop stop stop stop)

I was back in position for the final play when I realized something was wrong. Every muscle in my body had been burning with the intensity of play, but that heat vanished in an instant, as if I'd been dunked in liquid nitrogen. I froze up, almost literally. Then, something slithered inside me, itchy as it seeped into each and every pore. My skin stretched in all directions like a rubber band that would either snap back into place or snap in half. My agony lasted what felt like an eternity but must have only been a second. When my skin snapped back, it didn't return to its original shape. It hovered just above my muscles, impossibly suspended on a structure of nothing. My clothes felt tight around my swollen form, especially my shoes, which choked my feet blue.

I would have fled the field had the quarterback not thrown me the ball. Somehow, I caught it. And somehow, I ran through the defensive line, dodging opponents with unparalleled speed and grace. My feet carried me into the end zone and, arriving untouched, did a victory dance. I'd scored the occasional touchdown, but never with such ease and never with a victory dance to follow. After all, Mom, you taught me humility.

Eventually my feet stopped dancing and my teammates lifted me into the air. None of them commented on my new bulk, though it remained the only thought in my mind. They bounced me up and down, cheering my name. Silent, I pinched my arm to feel the empty space between skin and muscle. A restless wind circulated through my body's hollow. I pressed my ear to my forearm and listened to its whistle, its ecstatic howl.

My gaze drifted back to Coach. He was sitting just as before, his eyes closed in calm concentration, his white breath gentle as sleep. At first, I thought he'd actually dozed off. It was only when a player ran over to tell him we'd won that I realized he wasn't sleeping at all. Shouting in Coach's ear became shaking his shoulder became slapping his face. The man didn't stir.

But the wind inside me danced with joy, tickling my nerves from within. And that's when I screamed.

***

I had to take a break from writing, Mom. It's hard to revisit that time, especially knowing everything that came after it. But it's useless to mourn my lost years. Like you always said, the best cure for self-pity is action, and I have a plan. Is it stupid? Yes. Wrong?

Maybe. But it's something. SOMETHING THAT WILL NEVER WORK, SO DON'T EVEN THINK ABOUT IT. I MADE YOU AND I CAN DESTROY YOU.

(This is why I'm doing it. This is why I have no other choice.)

YOU WALK THE PATH OF THE FOOL.

(I walk the path of freedom.)

You remember how it went, Mom. Coach fell into a coma at that final game. The coma he's still in to this day. At least, that's what the doctors told Coach's sister who told ESPN. The doctors also said Coach's brain scans are unlike anything they'd ever seen before. They chalked it up to his previous head injury, but I don't buy it. I think something far stranger is at play, and for as long as the doctors try to understand it with science, answers will evade them.

The team visited Coach in the hospital every week until the end of the school year. I never joined, but it didn't matter. I was always with Coach in a way my teammates would never be. Some gave me shit for not visiting. I stopped talking to them after that, figuring it didn't matter if our friendships faded. My situation was impossible to explain without sounding insane, and we'd all go our separate ways after graduation anyway. Life would go on.

I soon learned a recruiter had seen my performance at that final game. When the scholarship letter came in the mail, I felt nothing, though the wind inside me danced for hours.

HOW COULD YOU FEEL NOTHING? UNGRATEFUL. UNWORTHY.

(I won't have to deal with this after today.)

I played three years of college football. Or rather, my body did, blown wherever Coach's wind fancied with me as its passenger. BLOWN TOWARD VICTORY. I also started sleepwalking again, but it wasn't like when I did it as a kid. I sometimes woke up to find myself bench pressing at the gym. It was always startling to open my eyes and find 250 pounds of iron hovering inches above my chest. I never got injured though. The wind made sure of that. It seemed to have infinite energy while I had none.

A mental fog stalked me through all my classes. I could barely process even the most basic accounting concepts, and more often than not, I fell asleep during class. Once, I woke up to an empty lecture hall. The class had ended and no one had bothered to wake me. I cried a little, then got ready for football practice. The wind took over after that, blowing with as much power as ever.

The only thing that could suppress it was a handful of oxy. Coach was addicted to the stuff, after all. Hell, so am I. The discovery was purely accidental. I sprained my ankle at practice, and a doctor wrote me a prescription for the pain. Those pills only lasted a week, but it was the most lucid week of my college career. After that, I spent most of my free, uncontrolled time searching for pills wherever I could find them. Any effort to salvage my academic career vanished.

But ultimately, it didn't matter that my grades were shit. My body played football so beautifully that the college let everything else slide. The NCAA would have come down hard on the athletic department, but my college coach thought the risk was worth the reward. For the three years I was there, our team won every college bowl game. We were unstoppable. THANKS TO ME. I remember seeing you in the stands at my last game before the Packers drafted me. You smiled and cheered and wore my same jersey. It broke my heart. I wanted to tell you about my pain, Mom. I've wanted to tell you for a long time. I just didn't know how.

***

LISTEN, MISS HOLZER. IF ANYONE IS THE VILLAIN HERE, IT IS YOUR SON. HE DEMONIZES THE MAN WHO MADE HIM A SUPERSTAR, THE MAN WHO SHOULD HAVE BEEN A SUPERSTAR HIMSELF, THE MAN WHO HAS NEVER RECEIVED CREDIT FOR HIS ACCOMPLISHMENTS.

REMEMBER WHEN YOUR SON PAID OFF YOUR HOUSE AND CAR? THAT WOULDN'T HAVE HAPPENED

WITHOUT ME. BUT THERE ARE STILL PLENTY OF DEBTS TO PAY, AREN'T THERE? I'VE HEARD HIM TALK ABOUT YOUR MEDICAL BILLS AND THE RUIN THEY'VE MADE OF YOUR RETIREMENT FUNDS. WOULDN'T IT BE NICE TO STOP SERVING AT RED LOBSTER 60 HOURS A WEEK? TO SIT BACK AND RELAX WITHOUT FINANCIAL WORRY? I SUSPECT I KNOW YOUR ANSWER.

JUST REMEMBER: IF YOUR SON GETS RID OF ME, HE'LL ONLY BE HARMING YOU.

****

I'm getting rid of him right after this entry. You probably won't see me again. Or if you do, it'll be behind bars. Ironic that prison is where I'll find my freedom. But I can't let him keep doing this. Even now, I feel his wind gusting inside me, trying to pin me down so I can't leave my home. But I just downed a few oxy. Well, more than a few.

Even with the sedation, I know he'll try to take control again when I get to the hospital. STOP. He'll try to make me turn back before I reach his room on the ninth floor. DON'T. He'll try to stop me from picking up a pillow and approaching his comatose body. YOU WOULDN'T. All I need is a few minutes of privacy and control. All I need is to press down hard. YOU'LL BE EMPTY WITHOUT ME. And maybe, just maybe, when that last breath leaves his body, his soul will leave mine. NEVER. I can only hope.

A Most Bulbous Congregation

(First published in *The Dead Inside*)

"… without the shedding of blood, there can be no forgiveness of sins." Hebrews 9:22, taken out of context as God intended

Wes expected the conversion therapy place to look like either a joyless summer camp or a clinic feigning medical legitimacy. The last two facilities his parents admitted him to had been exactly that. But this new one—third time's a charm—didn't pretend to be anything other than what it was: a crumbling church housing a crumbling ideology. A mile-long gravel driveway led to the building, which was coated in chipped white paint and surrounded by tall prairie grass. Under different circumstances, Wes might have found the sight beautiful. Sure, God didn't provide him any comfort, but he could appreciate the aesthetics of a steeple jutting high above the dancing yellow tips of bluestem. If only his father had brought him here on account of Wes's passion for photography —the one and only class he'd enjoyed in high school thus far. They'd have gotten some great shots and left the place feeling closer to each other. Alas.

His father parked in front of the church, a dust cloud settling behind the car. In the back seat, Wes reached into his pocket for his phone before remembering that his mother had snuck into his room and stolen it while he slept. Waking up to a vacant nightstand had clued him in to his parents' plans. Regardless of whether these places were summer camps, "medical" facilities, or churches, they all shared one rule: no phones. Whenever his phone disappeared, it meant another trip to Conversionville.

"Alright, Wes," his father said. He glanced briefly at his son in the rearview before averting his eyes. "I want you to take it seriously this time. It would mean a lot to me and your mother if … well, you know."

In the passenger seat, Wes's mother sniffled and squeezed her husband's hand. Wes wondered if she'd found something on his phone—a message from Taimoor he'd forgotten to delete. God forbid his boyfriend sent a risqué Snapchat, emboldened by the app's automatic delete-after-viewing feature. Maybe that's why Wes's mom cried the whole two-hour drive here. The church's heavy oak doors groaned open. Three people stepped out: an old man dressed in black priest vestments, a twenty-something woman in a blue dress that wouldn't look out of place in *Little House on the Prairie*, and a giant man in a tight long-sleeved button-up whose head scraped the door frame.

Wes's heart spiked at the sight of them. He stared into his lap as if looking away might make the trio disappear. But he had only a few seconds of pretending before his father opened the door and told him to get out. Wes sighed and did as he was told.

"Good morning, Mr. and Mrs. Hollis," the priest said. His low voice groaned like the church door, as if his vocal cords were made of the same ancient wood. He turned toward Wes in one robotically smooth motion. "And Wesley, a pleasure to meet you. I'm Father Michael. And these are my assistants, Mr. and Mrs. Warren. Happily married."

Wes wondered if the priest was insinuating the couple had been successfully "cured" of homosexuality. The more likely answer was that they were beards for one another, too deep in their roles to quit now: Mrs. Warren, the pioneer tradwife, and Mr. Warren, the masculine protector with the bulk of a rhino.

"Well, I see no reason to delay any further," Father Michael said. "Wesley, why don't you say goodbye to your parents? In two weeks' time, you'll return to them a saved boy. I'm sure you'll tick all the right boxes."

Mr. and Mrs. Warren exchanged a meaningful glance and chuckled. It was the first sound they'd made since the Hollis family arrived, and something about it made Wes's hair stand on end.

Lost in dreadful thought, Wes jumped when his mother embraced him. Her hold was tight and uncomfortably hot. He resisted the urge to squirm away. Then she whispered in his ear.

"I texted Tambor from your phone." *Taimoor. She means Taimoor,* Wes thought. But he wouldn't correct her with an "actually, my boyfriend's name is pronounced…" Instead, he held his breath for whatever would come next. A cold sweat ran down his neck.

"It was a break-up text. You understand, right, honey? Sometimes moms have to make tough decisions for their—"

Wes pulled away before the lump in his throat could escape as a sob.

"Okay." He looked down and kicked the dirt as if he were scraping dog shit off his shoe. "Bye, Mom. Bye, Dad." His father approached him. It looked like he might go in for a hug, but he paused at the last second, his eye twitching. *Are you scared of catching the gay, Dad? Getting infected with all the AIDS you probably think I have?* Wes trembled, his fists full of the same rage he'd felt when he punched Taimoor's bully in the face three months back. All it led to was a broken nose—Wes's broken nose, that is. He didn't care to repeat the experience. His father offered a hand. Wes shook it limply before pulling away and wiping his palm on his jeans. *You're scared of catching the gay, I'm scared of catching the bigot.* His father inhaled sharply and held it, the kind of breath that says a lot without needing words.

"Okay, let's go," he said.

Wes's parents got into the car and drove off. A white haze of dust obscured their departure. Wes thought of what he'd endure over the next two weeks, what he'd come home to when it was all done. He'd be no more straight, but he would be down one boyfriend, thanks to his mother. His soul ached. He wanted to stomp and cry and curse. All of this would've been endurable if Taimoor had been here with his dark sense of humor and willingness to openly mock authority figures.

Wes imagined what it'd be like to visit this gorgeous place under more romantic circumstances: a modeling session with no bigots present. Wes would snap pictures of Taimoor posing dramatically against the church door. It'd be the next entry in his "My Hot Boyfriend" photo series of the past six months. But this date existed only as a fantasy. Father Michael's voice dragged Wes back into reality.

"Shall we begin?" the priest asked.

His grin bore a malice greater than God.

***

A talk-therapy-slash-confession-session took up the next several hours. Wes had done this same exact thing at the clinic last year and the summer camp the year before that. He first tried lying in response to Father Michael's questions to make it seem like he was straighter than James Bond, but the priest's only response was, "Let's try that again, with honesty this time." The more he lied, the longer this bullshit would take. So Wes sat under the pink glow of the chapel's stained glass window, confessing to his first crush (King Triton from *The Little Mermaid*) and his occasional gay porn viewing (though not to his preference for straight-roommate-turned-gay scenes). He thought it was creepy the priest wrote down everything he said, nodding with what was either contemplation or relish. Would this information go back to Wes's parents? Into a priestly spank bank? The latter possibility both disgusted and saddened him.

Mrs. Warren entered the chapel around noon carrying a round silver tray of ham sandwiches, fruit salad, and water glasses with lemon slices adorning the rim.

"Lunch time," she said, her eyes as wide as the tray.

She set the meal on the altar between Wes and Father Michael. The sleeve of her pioneer woman dress pulled back with the motion, revealing a half-dozen scabs around her forearm. Some were crusted black while others leaked a clear pink fluid. Wes caught only a glance before Mrs. Warren pulled her sleeves back down, modest once more.

The priest looked down at the food, then up at Mrs. Warren with a question in his eyes. Mrs. Warren smiled and shook her head, then hummed her way back to the kitchen. Wes stared at Father Michael, attempting to interpret the odd interaction. The priest picked up a sandwich and raised it as if giving a toast before taking a bite. He chewed mechanically, as if keeping time with a metronome, and swallowed only when the food was an indistinguishable paste. At this rate, it'd take hours for him to finish the sandwich, but he put it down before the second bite.

"Sin lives in the blood," the priest said. "Did you know that?"

The shift in conversation caught Wes off guard. He wasn't sure if this was still part of the intake session.

"No, I didn't realize." It was all he could think to say. He hoped the priest would leave it at that.

"Christ's blood may be pure, but for the fallen, blood houses sin just as it houses oxygen."

Wes wondered if Father Michael was talking about AIDS. To keep himself from snapping, he took a big bite of his sandwich. Dry bread and overly salted ham. He didn't spit it out, but he wanted to—preferably in the communion chalice with Christ's most holy blood.

"Well." The priest gently lowered his hands to his thighs. "We've been talking a long time. How about a break before we come back? You're welcome to wander the grounds, though of course Mr. Warren will keep watch over you."

The air in the chapel was musty and hot in the July afternoon. Without saying another word, Wes walked out the door into the blinding prairie sea. He blinked at the sight of the sun in a cloudless sky. When his vision adjusted, he noticed Mr. Warren leaning beside the entrance and reading a Bible. The regular-sized book looked like a pocket version in the man's massive paw.

"Out for a walk?" Mr. Warren asked.

"Yes." Wes's voice cracked. He blushed and cleared his throat.

"Don't stray too far, and watch out for snake holes."

Mr. Warren went back to reading his Bible. The leather edges were well worn, and the pages were yellowed. It was a wonder the book didn't crumble in his grip. He didn't look up when Wes wandered off. Normally, Wes would take this as a chance to run, same as he had at the summer camp, but something told him looks were deceiving. In appearing to not watch, Mr. Warren was watching intently. And there was no way Wes could outrun him, not after skipping eighth period gym class for the past year so he could smoke with Taimoor away from the asshole jocks.

Wes eased into the prairie grass, letting his fingers brush against the scratchy seeded tops. A breeze whispered past him, its caress welcome in the blistering heat. He walked forward with his eyes closed, no destination in mind, no worry about snake holes. All he needed was sensation to ground him. Shuffling forward blind, he pictured the church burning behind him, sparks drifting and dying like fireflies in the night. He smiled.

A hiss from below. Wes jumped and covered his mouth when something grabbed his ankle. No, *someone*. It was Taimoor, crouched low in the tall grass. His tight tan shorts were filthy with dirt. Sweat fanned from the neck of his turquoise tank top. Four-inch, serrated sword earrings glinted against his brown skin. He smiled, and Wes tried his best not to react. But he'd stopped abruptly, and Mr. Warren had taken notice.

"You find one of those snake holes?" Even far off, the man's booming voice carried over the wind.

Wes turned his head to be sure the man wasn't following, then shouted, "No, just an interesting flower."

It was a bad lie, not to mention a gay one. He cringed and waited, but Mr. Warren didn't pursue the matter further. Wes lowered his head to look at Taimoor, making sure not to crouch too low.

"I'll play along," Taimoor said. "What kind of flower should I be?"

"Why are you here?" Wes spoke at barely a whisper. His expression alternated between creased worry and a smile he couldn't quite suppress.

"To fucking rescue you, of course. You told me the shit your parents pulled the last time they took you to one of these places, so when your mom texted me that you and I were breaking up—"

"How did you know it was her? She sent it from my phone."

"Would you use the phrase 'living in sin?'"

"Fair point. How'd you get here anyway? And how'd you find me?"

Taimoor squinted, pinched his nose, and muffled a sneeze like a bullet from a silenced gun. His allergies were bad enough that it was hard to go out in the summer. As romantic as it was to picnic at the park—and as necessary as it was given both Taimoor's and Wes's less-than-inviting homes—it was also a miserable sneeze fest. Wes wondered how many times Taimoor had suppressed sneezes in the hours he'd been waiting.

Taimoor continued: "I stole my dad's car. Tailed your parents here, but I think they might have seen me. I dunno. Maybe I'm being paranoid. But look, we can get out of here now, make a run for—fuck!"

Taimoor smacked his hand against the dirt as if he were beating the Earth to death.

The thudding, rustling noise was so obvious that Wes tried to cover it up by kicking the ground.

"Did something bite you?" he asked, remembering the snakes.

"A fucking tick," Taimoor said.

He held up his hand. A smear of blood decorated his thumb where the tick had latched. The juiced-up fucker scurried into the grass, well-fed and seemingly unharmed.

Mr. Warren shouted again: "Everything okay over there?"

"Yeah, just a…" Wes had no reason to lie this time. "Just a tick. That's all."

Mr. Warren laughed. It was the same unnerving laugh as before.

"How about you come in where it's safe," he said. It wasn't a question.

Wes glanced at Taimoor and whispered, "Tonight. The church doors." Taimoor frowned but nodded. They'd have a better chance at escape when it was dark anyway.

"I'll be a few hours straighter when you see me next," Wes said. He smiled despite the prickle of nerves.

Taimoor winked. "There'll still be plenty of gay left."

***

Wes didn't know if Taimoor had a plan beyond getting the hell out of there, but as the sun neared the horizon, he became increasingly confident that his boyfriend had things under control. Sure, a sneeze and some insect panic had nearly given Taimoor away, but that was how he rolled, embracing chaos and getting lucky in the end. Wes still remembered when Taimoor's mom caught them half-naked in the basement and Taimoor managed to convince her that shirtless study sessions were all the rage nowadays. She believed him, or at least didn't press the issue further. Wes didn't believe in God, but he had little doubt that some supernatural force protected Taimoor from the consequences of his actions. Hopefully that force would guide them tonight.

Wes spent the afternoon sitting in a pew beside Mr. Warren. It was this conversation that confirmed his earlier suspicions.

"I used to be like you," Mr. Warren said. His deep voice matched his massive frame, but somehow it sounded unconvincing, as if he were an actor cast in an ill-fitting role.

"You were gay?" Wes asked.

"A sinner, yes."

Wes fidgeted in the creaky pew. The angle made it hard to get comfortable. Mr. Warren's comment didn't help either.

"Father Michael cleansed me," Mr. Warren continued. "Cleansed the missus, too. He married us as soon as it was legal."

Mr. Warren's jagged teeth barely hid the hollowness behind his grin. Based on the man's baldness and wrinkles, Wes figured he was twenty years older than Mrs. Warren. He shivered at the thought that their marriage had probably been in the works long before she turned eighteen. But something on Mr. Warren's head drew Wes back to reality. He hadn't noticed it before, what, with the man towering a good two feet above him, but sitting side by side, it was easier to catch the bullseye-shaped rashes decorating his skull. Pink rings about two inches across surrounding dots that burned a deep, painful red. Mr. Warren noticed him noticing. He opened his mouth for a moment, then closed it and shook his head. Wes averted his eyes, more out of social courtesy than disgust. The church was silent save for the faint trilling of meadowlarks outside.

After a pause, Mr. Warren spoke: "Have your parents chosen your mate?"

Before Wes could respond, much less process, Mrs. Warren entered the room with another silver tray, her long dress trailing against the marble floor. Two bowls—one red and one blue—held a steaming beef stew. Beside them were slices of pumpernickel, each with a square pat of butter. Two tall glasses of iced tea dripped with condensation.

"Dinner has arrived," Mrs. Warren said.

She set the tray on the pew, then tapped a finger on her chin and chewed her lower lip.

"Something wrong?" Mr. Warren asked. His tone soured abruptly, sounding like a husband who smacked his wife when she cooked his steak wrong.

Mrs. Warren batted a hand in the air as if to say she'd figured out the problem, then flipped the tray around so the red bowl faced Wes and the blue bowl faced Mr. Warren.

She blinked too many times as she placed a hand on Wes's shoulder.

"The other one's bigger, you see," she said. "My husband, well … he might not be a growing boy anymore, but he's certainly a large man. Aren't you, dear?"

"Wesley and I were having a discussion," Mr. Warren said.

Wes sensed Mr. Warren's curtness wasn't in response to the size comment or the interruption, but he couldn't put his finger on what.

Mrs. Warren hurried out of the chapel. She disappeared into a side room and Wes heard a   lock click behind her. Silent, Mr. Warren eyed the meal the way one might eye a live octopus on a dinner plate.

"I'm not hungry," he said. "You can have mine, too."

"I'm good," Wes said. It was a lie, but something felt off.

Mr. Warren squinted at him like a predator assessing its prey. If Wes broke eye contact for even a moment …

"Let's talk about God's forgiveness," Mr. Warren said. "See —"

Wes couldn't take a second more of this shit. His stomach rumbled. He felt weak and lightheaded. Each word Mr. Warren spoke was a hammer pummeling his brain into mush. Maybe that's how they'd brainwash him. Exhaust him first, then rewire his zombified synapses. If he ate something, at least he'd have strength for his escape. Sure, Mr. Warren's reaction to the food had been strange, but maybe the guy was just picky.

Wes cut Mr. Warren off: "Actually, I am kind of hungry. Mind if we take a break so I can eat?"

Interrupting adults didn't normally end well for Wes. His mom would scold him, his teacher would give him the evil eye, and his dad … well, God forbid Wes ever interrupted him. Mr. Warren's reaction was different, though. The man smiled and nodded.

Wes tried to eat the stew slowly to delay further conversation, but the beef was so tender and savory that he wolfed it right down. Some mystery spice lingered just below the surface, exotic, irresistible, and like nothing he'd ever tasted. Given that he'd only had one bite for lunch, he tore into the second bowl after polishing off the first. Brown broth dribbled down his patchy chin, and Mr. Warren watched him with something like detached amusement. Wes pivoted away from the man to finish.

That's when he felt the pinch at the tip of his tongue. Had he bitten or burned himself? Had a sliver of bone escaped the meat and poked him? No, whatever it was clung to his tongue. Frowning, he pulled the thing, winced at its resistance, and finally plucked it loose. He held it in his palm—something small, black, and shiny, shaped like a teardrop. He poked it with his fork. It unfurled. Eight legs pulled out from the base and wriggled in a grotesque asynchrony. A tick. Wes threw the insect and dropped the bowl, which shattered on the scratched marble floor. When he stood up, his head was spinning. His eyes danced between ceramic shards, searching for the missing tick, but it only made him dizzier. He'd never been this off balance before. He gripped the pew for stability. It groaned when he swayed to one side, still unable to keep himself upright. Something was wrong.

Mr. Warren didn't get up. He hadn't moved once since the bowl broke. All he'd done was stare with those vacant eyes and that hollow smile. Wes tried to run when he saw the man's look. Fuck escaping tonight. He'd do it now. But his head felt like it was swimming with thick, heavy oil. Gray floaters crossed his vision, growing larger and darker each second. If he didn't get to Taimoor soon, he might not get another chance. Mr. Warren made no effort to chase him, possessing the nonchalance of a chess player ten steps ahead of his opponent. Wes staggered around a wooden column, then stumbled into the door Mrs. Warren had exited through. His hip cracked against the floor when he collapsed. Right then he knew his body would be unable to carry him to freedom. All he could do was scream for Taimoor and hope the boy heard. He howled his name again and again. But the weakness in his legs soon spread upward, his voice like a woodwind stripped of its reed. His neck bent at a harsh angle against the door, but it was this position that allowed him to hear what was on the other side: something dripping at a steady pace, and many somethings clicking together, as if Mrs. Warren were sifting through a bucket of glass beads. But even in that last sliver of consciousness, he knew the sound couldn't come from something so mundane, so harmless. He knew he'd meet whatever lay beyond that door if and when he awoke. And after shouting Taimoor's name, perhaps he would, too.

***

Wes awoke with his head full of blood. His skull felt like a water balloon close to bursting. His vision doubled and blurred, but a few blinks cleared it. The world was upside down with the pews looking as if they were on the ceiling. His body swayed gently, but even the slight movement upset his stomach. He puked half-digested stew into his nose, eyes, and hair. It dripped what appeared to be upward onto the lacerated marble floor. Wes shook the stinging, stinking puke from his eyes and twisted to see his feet. They were tied with a thin rope, connected to a pulley in the rafters. He wriggled his toes but felt no sensation. A moan escaped his lips.

"Ah, Wesley, you're awake," Father Michael said from below.

The priest held a communion chalice brimming with wine. Outside of Wes's vision came the rumble and screech of something heavy dragging across marble. Wes whipped his head around to see who else was there. Mr. Warren, bleeding profusely from his head, pushed pews toward the side of the room. Wes wondered how the man had been injured. His question was answered a moment later when his rope spun enough for him to see Mrs. Warren slapping a bound and gagged Taimoor in the corner of the room.

"Fucking stop it!" Wes said. Screaming sent another wave of dizziness through him, and he struggled to keep the rest of his lunch down. "Let us go! The cops will—"

He stopped, not confident the cops would do anything.

"My parents will—"

He stopped again for the same reason.

Taimoor managed to spit out his cloth gag. "*We'll* fucking kill you!" he said. "Me and Wes. We'll do it ourselves!"

"Shut up," Mrs. Warren said. Her second slap echoed through the chapel three times over. She reinserted Taimoor's gag, pushing it in deep with two forceful fingers. Taimoor choked audibly. "You don't get to talk after what you did to Mr. Warren."

Another sound—stone grinding against stone. Mr. Warren had widened the aisle between pews and was dragging something heavy into the space. Father Michael set down the communion chalice, grinning and grinding his teeth as he watched.

"Here it is," he said. "That which cleanses the sinner's blood. And how lucky we are to have two sinners with us today." He glanced at Taimoor. "God must have guided you here. All part of His divine plan." Taimoor let out a muffled scream through his gag. Wes thought it was in response to Father Michael's comment until he saw what Mr. Warren was dragging. A white circular tub big enough to fit four people. New gouges scarred the marble with each inch Mr. Warren dragged it. From afar, it could've been mistaken for an ornate hot tub, but it appeared to contain a sparkling black liquid. *They're tarring and feathering us*, Wes thought. But closer inspection revealed something worse. The black sparkles seemed to climb over each other, and despite the blood ringing a high pitch in Wes's ears, he could hear the same sound he'd heard before passing out: that awful clicking. Periodically, a glimmer of brown, red, or white would appear at the tub's surface only to sink once more under the blanket of wriggling black.

There was no denying it. The tick in Wes's stew hadn't been an accident, a lone bug outside its natural habitat. No, this church was a sanctuary for the armored, the eight-legged, the bulbous. Here, and nowhere else, they were loved and worshipped.

The tub of ticks scraped to a halt directly below Wes. He let out something between a sob and a scream.

"And now, to cleanse you," Father Michael said.

He grabbed a crank connected to the pulley and gave it several turns, lowering Wes toward the tub. The priest's breath was ragged, as if the simple task of cranking might make him keel over. He was a frail, pathetic man. If Wes and Taimoor hadn't been tied up, they'd have made easy work of him. Wes imagined tossing the priest in his own "cleansing" tub and watching the ticks suck him down to a desiccated jerky.

But there was no time to entertain fantasy. Wes thrashed and howled and searched for anything to aid in his escape. The pulley system groaned. Taimoor sobbed and cursed through his gag. Father Michael sang in Latin, his voice off-key and grating, as Wes found all priests' voices to be. Approaching the tub, Mr. Warren joined with his tuneless baritone and Mrs. Warren with a crisp, bright soprano. Wes's ears throbbed. So did his head. His *everything*. He attempted to do a crunch to reach his bound feet, but two tries were enough to know it wouldn't happen. He panted, exhaustion and adrenaline at war with each other. There was nothing he could do. Just a few more feet and he'd be bathing in ticks. Had his parents known this was the plan all along? The possibility was too painful to consider.

The hideous hymn grew louder. Wes jerked his body to face Taimoor. If he was going to die, he wanted to see the love of his life one last time. But where he expected to find bittersweet sorrow, he instead found hope. Taimoor had removed one of his sword-shaped earrings to saw loose his bindings. Wes had warned Taimoor not to wear them given how dangerously sharp they were, but now he was glad Taimoor had ignored him.

Three feet to go. Below Wes, the ticks crawled over each other in an orgy of bloodlust. Wes pictured the biggest among them sinking to the bottom, large as fists and brimming with a queer teen's drained lifeforce. How many others had come before Wes? He pressed his chin to his chest to put more space between himself and the ticks. He grunted with exertion and glanced at Taimoor again. When Mrs. Warren noticed him looking elsewhere and turned to follow his eyeline, Wes shrieked—half performance to distract her and half genuine expression of terror. The woman returned her attention to Wes and smiled as she sang, her lips forming large, exaggerated shapes for each vowel: "Ixodes! Sanguis! Purgo!"

Father Michael stopped singing, but the Warrens continued to the next verse.

"After you are drained," the priest rasped, cranking with one hand and grabbing the communion chalice with the other, "you will drink Christ's blood and let it replace the impure with the pure. This is your first step to forgiveness, to salvation."

There were mere inches between Wes's head and the ticks. But his savior was coming, and it wasn't Jesus. Taimoor's legs were still bound, but his arms were free now. He hopped forward as silently as possible, a sword earring in each hand. And then Wes felt it. A tickle in his scalp, intensifying and crawling upward. His eyes were level with the tub's rim. He'd plunge into it screaming with a lungful of ticks at any moment.

That's when Taimoor struck. Mr. Warren's singing became screaming as Taimoor leapt onto the giant's shoulders and plunged the sword earrings into his eyes. Blood spurted in fountainous arcs. Mr. Warren flailed, but Taimoor clung to him like a rodeo rider. Mrs. Warren shrieked and Father Michael stepped away from the crank.

"Degenerates! Murderers!" the priest howled.

When Mr. Warren stopped thrashing, Taimoor let go. The giant collapsed like a felled redwood. His skull hit the marble with an echoing crack. He didn't get back up.

Though the rope hadn't lowered any farther, the ticks still swarmed Wes's face. They waded through crusting trails of puke, hunting for a vein hot with the boy's blood. Ticks clambered over one another for a drink of what, to them, was only ever a meal, never a sin. Hundreds punctured Wes's skin and sucked. He screamed as the warmth left his face. Mrs. Warren slapped and screamed at Taimoor, but Wes couldn't discern her slurred, vicious words through the ticks flooding his ears. All he heard was a gasp, *crunch*, and then silence. Mrs. Warren never spoke again.

"How dare you!" Father Michael said. His voice was loud and clear enough to carry. "The little ones will purify your rotten—"

"Shut the fuck up!" Taimoor said. Father Michael let out an *oof*, but Wes couldn't see what was happening through the writhing black. On cue, Taimoor brushed Wes's cheek, scooping the ticks away as if his hand were a squeegee. With the priest moaning on the floor and still very much alive, they had little time to waste. Taimoor ripped away the ticks along with patches of skin and hair. Wes yelped and cried, though he knew it had to be done.

"I'm getting you down," Taimoor said, then kissed Wes's oozing lips.

"Sinners!" Father Michael screamed.

Wes could see the man now as he staggered to his feet.

"Back the fuck up!" Taimoor said, wielding his sword earrings.

The sight of such tiny swords would've been laughable had he not just used them to gouge a man's eyes out. Father Michael stepped back. It appeared as if he might cooperate, but then he grabbed the crank and spun it wildly. The man knew his death was imminent; he'd purify one last sinner on his way out. Only, it didn't work. As the priest cranked, Taimoor pulled Wes's head toward the edge of the tub until, finally, he was fully outside it. The ticks could no longer reach him.

"To Hell with you!" Father Michael said.

Taimoor ignored the man as he untied Wes's bindings and picked loose the last few ticks. Wes's vision blackened as he stood. Feet feeling as if they were made of wet sand, he lurched forward in a struggle for stability.

"I'll grab the priest," Taimoor said. "Come over when you're ready."

Father Michael resisted as much as an old man could, but Taimoor pinned him down with ease. He recoiled at Taimoor's touch like a possessed person recoiled at holy water.

"Unhand me, faggot!" the priest said.

"Wes, come on!" Taimoor said. "I'm fucking sick of this creep."

Wes rounded the tub like something out of a nightmare, his face a bloody mess pocked with a thousand raised red dots.

"Lift him up," Wes said.

Taimoor did so, gripping Father Michael by his armpits. The priest launched into prayer.

"Oh heavenly Father, may your light guide and protect me against—"

Wes didn't care to listen. Expression blank, he turned to his boyfriend. Taimoor nodded, then shifted to the priest's left side, allowing Wes to take the right. Together, they dragged him toward the tub. Father Michael ended his prayer prematurely.

"Fools!" he said, trying and failing to maintain the illusion of control. "The little ones only feast on the impure. They'll find none of me to their liking. It's useless to even—"

They reached the tub's rim. Frenzied clicking and skittering escalated in anticipation of the next meal. The priest stared at his little ones with the whites of his eyes on full display.

"On my count," Wes said, and Taimoor readied himself.

Father Michael wept as three became two and two became one. Wes and Taimoor lowered him into the tub headfirst. The black surface seethed as he sank. Weeping became screaming, but his terror didn't last long. His little ones were there to comfort him for the very last time.

***

"You're shaking," Taimoor said as Wes climbed into the stolen car.

It was dark now save for the red glow a mile off. The prairie would probably catch fire soon if it hadn't already. For that—and only that—Wes felt bad. He pulled his arms around his chest and didn't bother with the seatbelt.

"We just killed people," he said.

"Well, yeah, but … yeah, we did," Taimoor said. He started the ignition, then caressed Wes's tense shoulder.

"I need a fucking shower."

"Yeah, you do. You smell like a rotting corpse in a dump truck."

"Thanks." A half-smile crept onto Wes's face, then vanished when he felt something crawling on his neck. He slapped the spot but found nothing. Whether it was a tick that got away or his traumatized imagination acting up, he couldn't be certain.

"We should go," he said. "Somewhere I can wash off, preferably."

"Right." Taimoor shifted the car into drive. "I'll see what I can find."

They took off down the country road, flying into the night. Wes had no idea what their destination would be, but he trusted his boyfriend. As long as they were together, whether in joy or suffering, things would turn out fine. He had no choice but to believe it.

THE LAST SUMMER

Bad things happen when summer camp counselors have sex. Sometimes the vengeful mother of a drowned boy murders them mid-thrust. Other times they finish (or one of them does) only to find the campers slashed to bits in their cots. Sex equals death. It's a horror movie rule at this point.

Alec and I were the exception. When we made love the last night of Camp Holly, neither of us died. At least I don't *think* Alec died. But the memory still haunts me, dripping into my mind like dark ichor in lonely hours.

I knew Alec's camp counselor name before I ever knew him as Alec. It was a camp expectation that all counselors name themselves after a tree. Alec wanted to go with "Baobab," but the kids couldn't pronounce it, so he went with "Oak" instead. I chose "Elder," half because it was funny with me being only eighteen but also because it was close to my actual name, Elden. Even when Alec and I made out behind the boathouse, he insisted on calling me Elder. It was his way of flirting. I handed it right back by calling his cock "Oak." These moments of play carried a spark of magic, and when Alec gazed at me with that crooked smile, his body shimmered and ceased to be entirely real. I used to pass it off as a trick of the eyes, swimming with starlight desire, but now I know better.

Our late-night hookups meant we were both tired during morning crafts, but supervision duty wasn't that difficult. When the kids had art supplies in front of them, they could mostly take care of themselves. Alec and I would watch with shoulders pressed together from the shade of a pine tree, our affection obvious to anyone with eyes. The kids twisted pipe cleaners into horses, elephants, and dragons. Those twiggy creatures became friends and so did their makers. Bonding campers planned to meet up during the school year, but of course, that wasn't how camp worked. One day they'd understand the illusion of summer's promise—its beauty and its cruelty.

Somehow, I got it in my head that Alec and I were exempt from reality. While supervising, we often whispered about what life together would be like after camp ended. Only once did a kid overhear our conversation and say something about it. "Are you two gay?" he asked. The snot dripping from his nose saved me from answering. I directed him to a tissue box on a picnic table, and he scurried off. Alec and I went on planning our future.

We'd get a studio apartment in Philly where he could paint and I could study for bio exams. College wouldn't be easy, but I'd make time for us. When Alec wasn't painting commissioned portraits of people's cats and I wasn't serving guests at the Olive Garden, we'd spend time exploring abandoned lots, drinking two-dollar wine straight from the bottle, and watching pirated horror movies late into the night. It'd be an existence meager in luxury but abundant in love.

Then again, what use was planning for a future that never came? Sometimes imagination breeds only pain, an arthritis of the soul aching with unfulfilled desire. I don't fault myself for getting carried away though. I couldn't have predicted how our story would end.

It was the last night of camp and the kids were asleep in their cabins. At first light, I'd head back to Pittsburgh and Alec would return to Allentown. It'd be another month before we moved to Philly together, so we did what any couple with one night left together would do—made sweet gay love under the full moon, as God intended. The trees gave us cover: maple, cedar, and ash, but only one Oak, only one Elder. Alec whispered my nickname as he entered me. I relished his fullness, how he was big but always gentle. The cicadas buzzed a comforting drone. A stiff wind hissed through the trees. I shivered, pulled my arms around my bare chest. Tree sap and flakes of bark clung to my skin.

"Hold me," I said.

Alec's embrace was warm, as if it had retained all the sun he'd soaked up the past two months. His pumping continued at a steady pace, and his panting was a pleasant tickle on my neck. I felt myself getting harder, closer.

And then, with arms still around me, Alec froze.

"Are you about to——?" I stopped.

Something was off. Alec wasn't losing warmth so much as he was losing opacity. In the dappled moonlight, his arms were paralyzed and fading, tanned coils of muscle going translucent. I no longer felt his heart pounding against my sweaty back. It was as if someone had hit the pause button on his pulse and dimmed his existence with a fader switch. Though he hadn't pulled out of me, I felt myself close up around his dwindling. I wanted to scream, but I didn't want to draw attention. I wanted to squeeze his arms and bind him to Earth, but he looked as if he were made of glass. I couldn't bear to shatter him.

When he vanished, a cloak of cold wind swallowed me. I sobbed, hand over mouth, drifting naked and aimless through the grove. I called his name once, twice, hoping either he would appear or I would disappear with him. He never returned. I remained chained to existence.

I put my clothes on and returned to the cabin. While the campers snored in their bunks, I stared glass-eyed at the ceiling until morning.

Eventually, the breakfast bell rang. The yawning kids left the cabin and migrated to the cafeteria. I dragged my feet behind them, wondering who I could tell about last night. Not the other counselors and definitely not my parents.

After breakfast, they came to pick me up, approaching the tree-lined shore in their SUV. I said nothing on the drive home, just told them I was tired. They left me to nap in the back seat, my head rattling against the window.

A week later, I looked up Alec's parents on social media. I expected to find pleas for information about their missing son, but instead I found his mother's photos of her blooming hydrangeas and his father's rant about the ending of some show called *Believed*. It was as if their son had never existed, as if they'd just moved on after he didn't come home.

Now, whenever the cicadas buzz, I think about that last summer, about the future Alec and I planned and lost together. All we ever had was a wink and dream. I wonder if I'll ever have anything more.

ELEVATOR BOYS

It wasn't Garrett's fault Evan fell down the elevator shaft, but he blamed himself anyway.

We discovered the place during a post-trick-or-treat urban exploration. This was the era when parents told their kids to go outside and stop bothering them—*just be home for dinner.* We climbed through the condemned housing project's lowest broken window, then took the crumbling concrete stairs six floors up, navigating without flashlights. Glass crunched underfoot—a beer bottle or syringe. Other times the detritus was a squishy, sour-smelling mystery.

"I bet all my candy that was one was a turd," Raymond said, scraping the gunk off his shoe.

"Nah, it's gotta be a dead rat," Evan said. "Probably a ton of those in here."

We never found out because that's when Garrett pointed out the elevator, its metal jaws opened at a slant, beckoning.

We took turns peeking down the shaft, shouting "penis" and listening as the word plunged six stories and then echoed back up. It made us giggle every time. The bottom remained cloaked in shadow. Our only light came from the hallway's cracked window, moon spilling through swirling clouds of mold and asbestos. When shouting "penis" got boring, Raymond and I—the mature ones— hung back. We fumbled blindly through our candy bags, hunting for Reese's peanut butter cups. I popped one in my mouth and let the wrapper drift to the carpet of trash below.

Had the city torn down this abandoned building, Evan might have lived to see another Halloween. But ironically, the holiday played a part in his death. It was that damn dollar store vampire cape. He'd tripped over it a hundred times while we were trick-or-treating, leaving the end mangled and dusty—much more Dracula-like than it had looked straight out of the package. If only he'd taken it off for convenience's sake. But Evan always committed to his role: on Halloween, in games of cops and robbers, in the elementary school play.

While Raymond and I ate candy, Evan and Garrett stood together at the elevator opening, howling like wolves. The echo was deafening, as if a whole pack were at the bottom. I smiled and, with a mouth full of chocolate, joined the joyful racket. Even Raymond, who normally told us to shut up when we were being loud, let out a howl.

What happened next has never left my memory. Garrett was first to hear the beating of bat wings. He yelped and jumped backward as a hundred dark shapes zipped out of the elevator and into the hallway. Garrett's sudden motion threw Evan off balance and he windmilled his arms to stay upright. That's when his cape caught under his foot for the final time. Following our fading howls was a breathless whoosh, a violent frenzy of wings, a metallic crash.

And then he was gone.

***

That building stayed up. Evan's parents wrote countless letters to the mayor begging him to demolish it, but the city didn't have money. They only made room in the budget when the same thing happened to Garrett three years later.

Garrett, Raymond, and I visited the building every Halloween to pay our respects. We never told our parents. The building deteriorated from one year to the next. A dozen more graffiti artists had used it as a canvas, and just as many squatters had used it as a bathroom. The smell made us gag, but we never turned back.

That first Halloween after Evan's death, we stood beside the mouth of the elevator in silence. Then, unprompted, Raymond stepped forward, pulling all the Reese's out of his bag.

"These are for you, Evan," he said, and dropped them down the shaft.

I followed suit, making my own offering. For a few seconds, we heard only the dull whistle of a wind tunnel. But then came the chewing. The sound continued for a minute, wet and loud and crinkling, as the Reese's were devoured, wrapper and all. It terrified me at first, but eventually I found comfort in the chewing. It was as if Evan were sitting next to me in the school cafeteria.

When Garrett dumped his Reese's, it was different. There was never any chewing, never the feeling that Evan had pulled up to the table smiling, his lunchbox loaded with candy. Garrett shouted down the shaft to see if Evan was full, but no voice responded—not even Garrett's own echo. There was only an all-consuming silence.

He tried again the next Halloween, insisting he make the first offering, but the response was the same. He didn't talk for a week after that.

Then came the third try. Same as before, Raymond and I made our offerings, and just as usual, the thing in the elevator shaft accepted them. I couldn't be sure it was Evan, but I liked to think it was. When I asked Garrett if he could hear the chewing, he shook his head and drew in a long, shuddering breath. His arms trembled like they did when he drank too many Cokes at a sleepover. I thought about putting a hand on his shoulder but decided against it.

When the chewing ended, Raymond and I stepped away from the elevator shaft. Garrett approached, his breath shallow and fast. He opened his candy bag, but instead of just offering the Reese's, he dumped his entire haul. The pieces tumbled down the shaft, pattering against its sides. Raymond winced like he did whenever I told a joke and no one laughed. I stared at my feet and closed my eyes. When a minute passed without any chewing, a different sound cut through the darkness: a zipper, then a steady stream of water. Tensing, I looked up.

"Is this what you want, Evan?" Garrett shouted, pissing down the shaft. "What do I have to do to—"

Raymond grabbed Garrett's shoulder to pull him back, but Garrett whipped around for a haymaker. His fist skimmed Raymond's ear, but the momentum carried him in an uncontrolled circle. I knew what was about to happen, and given how wide his eyes were, Garrett did too. I tried to catch his shirt as he fell backward, but I was too late.

This time there were no flitting bats. Only Garrett's scream—high and long and sad—and the crunch of his body breaking. I would've screamed too, but one final sound paralyzed me: chewing. No longer chocolate and plastic crinkling between teeth, but tendons and bones snapping between jaws.

***

The next day, while the adults ran around and made tear-choked phone calls, Raymond and I stayed in my bedroom. The police had just questioned us, taking me to the backyard and Raymond to the front porch. They made me tell them exactly what happened to Garrett five times, though the details I gave them —mostly honest—never changed. Eventually, they let me go and I retreated to my room. Raymond was already sitting on my bed with wet eyes and a sniffly nose.

"Do you think it was him?" he asked.

"What? Who do you mean?"

"Evan. The chewing. After Garrett—"

I shook my head. "No. I can't believe he'd do that."

But maybe people change when they die. Maybe the dead crave vengeance.

Dead Rain

(First published by Dread Stone Press)

Four ghosts don't cut it anymore. My ancestors swirl fog-like and cool the air above our farm, but the world's gotten too hot for rain again. Adding another ghost should fix that for a while, get us a couple good downpours before the growing season is out. The question is whether it will be me or Dad.

When I volunteer for the job at supper, Dad scowls up at me from his plate of literal roadkill. A forkful of skunk clatters to the table.

"You stupid?" he asks.

"No, I'm brave," I say, but my voice cracks.

Dad shakes his head. His nose wrinkles when he looks back at his meal. He scoops what's left onto my plate.

"Eat up," he says. "You're a growing boy."

His message is clear: soon only one of our mouths will need feeding.

***

I steal Dad's rusty shotgun from his closet. He hasn't used it since that knife-wielding thief came looking for a meal and became one instead. The barrels taste bitter in my mouth, but better than that man by far. Dad should never have to make that decision again, to hear his gut rumbling and think *meat is meat.* I want him to enjoy the corn, beans, and tomatoes of years past. Dad claims it used to rain so hard, the tomatoes would swell 'til they split. Just one would fill you up for the whole day, and there were plenty to go around. Add another ghost and Dad could have that again.

But my trigger finger hesitates. Seconds become minutes and before I know it, Dad is busting into the shed, smashing the shotgun on the floor, and slapping me across the cheek.

"It's not your responsibility, Aiden!" he says, eyes glassy in the moonlight. "Now go to bed."

The shotgun barrel is twisted and its stock is cracked in half. At least Dad won't be able to kill himself once I leave. At least not without a little creativity.

In bed, I stare out the open window. Our family ghosts rotate in ceaseless circles. I try talking to Mom, but she just keeps churning. A breeze blows in as if from Hell itself, and I sweat myself to sleep.

***

Roadkill is sparse nowadays. Fewer trucks barreling down dirt roads with country music blaring and even fewer deer jumping in front of said trucks. Still, Dad and I leave the farm early each morning and walk for miles, hoping we'll stumble upon something edible. We hunt with our noses as much as our eyes, sniffing out animal rot and scanning the sky for buzzards.

We haven't found anything in three days.

"Drink up." Dad passes me his beat-up metal water bottle.

Even with sweat stinging my eyes and July heat boiling my skin, I take only the smallest sip. The shotgun failed me, but maybe dehydration will do the trick. If I'm lucky, I'll collapse in our front yard and croak under the willow tree of my childhood, stripped of its shaggy leaves but weeping nonetheless. I picture drifting through the night sky with Mom, Granddad, Uncle Louis, and Aunt Melissa, our collective cold chilling the air enough to bring rain, crops, and a future for Dad. But thinking about rain only makes me thirstier. I cap the water bottle before I can drink what my body needs.

When I pass it back, Dad pauses, weighing it in his hand. He squints as if he knows what I'm trying to do, but he doesn't press me on it.

We walk past the Hendersons' ranch, littered with bones both bovine and human. Death claimed that plot years ago, but the stench remains. Dad and I climb over downed electrical poles and cut through a cornfield baked into lifeless tinder. The highway is just beyond. Hopefully somewhere on its scorching, crumbling blacktop, we'll find a meal.

We see one immediately: an unarmed, emaciated man staggering down the road and moaning. His face is a nest of yellow boils and his tennis shoes look a dozen steps away from disintegrating. Blood-red sunburns cover every inch of his skin. I imagine peeling the boiled layers away and finding nothing but bone underneath.

Before the man can notice us, we slink back into the cornfield. Dad looks at me, unblinking, with that horrible question in his eyes. Last time the choice was easy. When a man kicks in your door and pulls a knife on your son, a father does what he must.

This time is different. I picture Mom observing from above as we choke this defenseless man to death, neck blisters bursting under the force of our grip. The time I stole a cow from the Hendersons, Mom screamed that I was a boy of little honor. I can't imagine what she'd say about me squeezing the life from a suffering man. But she's always silent, no matter how many times I beg for her guidance. Maybe she'd abandon Earth for the next world after witnessing our cold-blooded survivalism, the air above our farm a few degrees hotter in her absence.

Dad's still staring, wanting me to make the call. The man stumbling down the scorching highway lets out an agonized sob. Maybe he's begging to be put out of his misery, but I can't let my assumption become a reason to kill. I won't be Mom's boy of little honor.

I shake my head "no." We go home hungry.

***

A week with nothing to eat. No skunk. No thief. No howling drifter. I can count my ribs now. The ghosts can, too. They're spinning faster, desperate to bring rain and even the most modest of crops.

Dad's locked himself in his room to fix his shotgun, but I can't let him end it for my sake. I could never live with the guilt, especially alone.

I remember the knife the thief pressed to my throat. We kept it after Dad killed him. Dizzy with hunger, I press a hand against the wall and shuffle to the kitchen. I'll feel that knife against my flesh one final time.

Dad will thank me later.

A Coarse Yellow Sea

(First published in *Hell Is Real: A Midwest Gothic Anthology*)

Maybe I'll be dead by the time you read this, Darren. Hell, farmers and suicide go together like steak and potatoes. I might as well do it before the court commits me. But I wanted to write to you first.

I know you noticed my blush when we talked. You probably assumed it was nervousness because it's easier to be friends with an anxious man than a homo. After what happened with my son, you probably think I'm worse than a homo now. But please, listen to my story, try to understand me, and if you have it in your heart, do me one last kindness.

When Aiden was still alive, he helped out around the farm, feeding cattle and scooping their shit. I worked him until dusk most days, but he didn't complain. The boy didn't have any friends, and the neighbor kids a mile off were too young. I'd like to think the work kept him from feeling lonely, same as it did for me.

Thing is, Aiden got lazy after finding his passion for dressage. I always thought it odd he chose that over rodeo—a much more exciting sport, in my humble opinion—but it didn't bother me. What really ground my gears was how he'd sneak away from shit-scooping duty to train his horse, Gus. A week back, I caught them behind the barn practicing pirouettes for the county fair. There were worse things he could've been doing—following his mother's footsteps straight to jail—but the blistering July heat made me snap. Tough love was in order, though now I wish I'd settled for the gentler variety. Something like, *Real excited for your competition, son. You and Gus'll do great. Listen, how 'bout you scoop a little more poop, then get back to training?* But no, I wasn't that kind.

"Tie up your damn horse and follow me," I said.

Aiden's sigh boiled my blood. I would've expected it from a spoiled city kid but not from my son. I'd planned to assign him an extra few stalls to scoop, but I decided to throw in something extra. Something that'd put a little fear in him.

We walked to the silo, which had been clogged since morning. There were safe ways to unclog it, but I had only one method in mind for Aiden: walking the grain down. My father had me do it as a kid before OSHA saw the method's dangers and declared it illegal. I'd walk across the grain's shifting surface and hope the clog would clear before the grain swallowed me like quicksand. Nothing bad ever happened, but I often woke in the middle of the night feeling like my lungs were full of silage: hot, prickly, and suffocating. My father knew the job scared me, but he never offered an alternative. It was how we'd always done things. Come to think of it, no philosophy has done more harm to the world than that one.

Aiden didn't complain when I told him to walk down the grain. He just nodded, dropped his gaze, and climbed into the silo. Silage rustled as it tumbled down. Several minutes passed. I leaned against the steel auger, one hand scratching my beard and the other swatting horseflies. I'd love to say I had second thoughts about Aiden's punishment, but truth be told, my mind was elsewhere.

Aiden's mother was three years incarcerated, and we hadn't spoken in just as long. While we weren't legally divorced, my eye couldn't help but wander. I blushed whenever I talked to Marlene, that pretty woman working the Rushville gas station. And strange as it sounds, even you stirred up longings when you came over to buy silage. I wasn't sure if this fondness for men came from my dry spell or if it had always been lurking under the surface.

I didn't much care to ponder it.

A scream tore me from my thoughts but was cut short just as soon. I froze, sure I'd hallucinated. But the trickle of grain and absence of footsteps made my hair stand on end. I scrambled up the silo ladder and looked inside. Aiden was gone, swallowed up in a coarse yellow sea.

I jumped in after him, skirting the metal edge to avoid sinking myself. I scanned for any sign of him—his protruding hand or navy blue cowboy hat—and found nothing. I shuffled closer to the silo's center. My left foot sank into the grain, but that didn't matter. I shouted Aiden's name and dug through the silage, tossing handfuls of grain back toward the wall. When I stopped sinking at the ankle, I wondered if I was standing on him. I searched below, crying and screaming and hot in the face. It was a good ten minutes of that before I realized too much time had passed.

Eventually I climbed out of the silo, but now I wish I'd stayed there. Wish I'd followed him.

***

Of course, it's impossible to hide that kind of secret for long. You pieced the clues together eventually.

Aiden remained at the bottom of the silo. Or at least his body did. I didn't care if the grain spoiled so long as it hid him from view. He'd get a proper burial when I was ready to face what I'd done.

It won't surprise you that I distracted myself with work. Without Aiden's help, I had plenty more to do. I found if I toiled sixteen sweltering hours without so much as a lunch break, I became too exhausted to dwell on my emotions. Sleep came easy, but so did nightmares. Just like in childhood, I dreamt I was drowning in grain, rough silage tickling my neck as it swallowed me. The only difference between these nightmares and the ones from long ago was the sound. Two screams instead of one: mine and Aiden's, a shared terror as we suffocated together. Except I woke up alive in a sweat and Aiden didn't. At least I don't think he did. Like I said, boy isn't quite dead. And before you start assuming I'm either denying it or losing my mind, hear me out.

Three days in, I realized I hadn't tended to Gus. Aiden had always been the one to care for his horse, so you can't blame me for forgetting. Still, the realization put a feeling in my gut like I'd sucked down a dozen lemons. I'd let one of the last remnants of my son go three-days mad with thirst and hunger. It was a wonder I hadn't heard him neighing, thrashing, and kicking his metal stall.

Silage was the only suitable food I had for him. Using my own tainted grain felt wrong, but the supply store in town was out of stock until the end of the week and letting Gus starve wasn't an option. Returning to the silo felt like stepping back into that nightmare. I closed my eyes as the auger hummed and extracted grain. Though I tried to suppress the thought, I imagined Aiden tumbling from the auger, limb by broken limb, his head emerging last with a stare of gray, eternal judgment. When I opened my eyes, there was no Aiden, but the unloaded silage had an odd, rusty hue. I tried not to think about where it came from as I fled, full bucket in hand.

I found Gus laying on his side in the stable. He snorted and lolled his head when he saw me, the yellowed whites of his eyes on full display. I couldn't tell if my approach comforted or terrified him, but he readily devoured the rust-colored grain when I held it out. As he chewed, his dry lips brushed my fingers. I scratched his nose with my free hand, but he nuzzled it away and returned to his food. There was no love here. Only hunger.

Then, Gus's eyes changed. That's how it looked, anyway: black pupils expanding, yellowed whites bleaching, jittery panic dissolving into unnerving calm. I think that was the moment Aiden's soul found its new body. Wouldn't blame you for thinking I'm full of shit, but do a grieving man a favor and keep reading.

After Gus ate himself to bloat and chased it down with ten gallons of water, I took him for a ride. Maybe it was wrong to ride him in his weakened state, but I wanted his companionship.

Anyone's companionship, really. Like any good horse, Gus never bucked or ran off; he only did what Aiden told him. And sure, I wasn't Aiden, but I'd ridden Gus on many occasions without issue.

This time was different. He was calm when I mounted him, as if he'd been expecting it. I brushed his tangled mane, then tapped the stirrups to get him moving. That was when he threw me. He was completely silent as he reared—no wild, drawn-out neigh like you'd hear in a Hollywood Western. I reached for his reins too late and crashed to the ground. The fall knocked the wind out of me and sent up a dust cloud. I coughed, wheezed, and hacked yellowish spit down my chin. Gus rotated to face me, but he didn't stomp or snort or bare his teeth. I scrambled backward, sure he'd charge. Instead, he gazed at me with placid, unblinking eyes. His stare lasted an eternity. It felt as if I were sinking underwater, the pressure building, crushing and unbearable.

Just as I crumpled, Gus walked away, leaving me like roadkill not even a vulture would eat. Calm as a windless night, he ambled toward the pasture, taking no interest in the grass and not bothering to swat away the swarming flies. He just moved forward and stared at the horizon as if earthly matters no longer concerned him.

"Gus!" I called out.

His ears didn't even twitch. He kept moving.

"Whoa, Gus, whoa!"

He didn't stop. It was as if someone had replaced him with an identical-looking but totally untrained horse.

An insane notion bubbled up inside me. I clenched my jaw but found myself unable to suppress the next word.

"Aiden!"

Gus stopped but didn't turn around. I held my breath. The horse remained still for only a moment. He lingered a second longer, then shuffled off like a soul trapped between Heaven and Earth.

***

You visited the day after Aiden bucked me. I'd mentally prepared myself to retrieve his body that morning, but you drove up in your old truck before I could. When you hopped out, you were wearing a sweat-darkened Huskers hat and a green flannel rolled up to the elbows. You nodded at me as you walked up the gravel drive. I hadn't showered in days and had completely forgotten you'd be visiting.

"Hey, John," you said. "You look about two coffee pots short of a good morning."

I struggled to find words but was grateful you had offered the seed of a lie.

"Slept like shit." My voice cracked. For a moment, I wondered if Aiden had possessed me and not his horse. I cleared my throat. "How are, uh, things in your world?

"Not bad," you said, pulling a dip tin from your jeans and tucking a wad under your lip. "Did some back-to-school shopping with Ellen this morning. Guess she and Aiden have the same algebra class. Your boy's welcome to study over at our place sometime."

Slack-jawed, I nodded, fixating on the ground. My eyes felt close to boiling over.

"Listen, I can tell you're busy," you said. "How about we load some silage into my truck real quick and you can get on with your day?"

I imagined Aiden's limbs, gray and rotted and peppered with grain, tumbling out of the auger, rust-colored silage piling up around them. Pictured you and I both screaming.

"About that," I said. "I … I'm all out."

The terrible lie came out as a rasp. I glanced up. You frowned and scratched your sunburnt neck. Droning cicadas filled the thick silence.

"Well, guess I'll see if Charles has some," you said. "I'll come back next week though. Think you'll have any then?"

"No," I said, then winced at my response. "I'm … I'm sorry, Darren. It's just—"

"You okay, John?" you asked.

Your words bore gentleness rather than confrontation. I always appreciated that about you, how you treated me kindly as far back as elementary school, helping me up after the other boys beat my ass. But when you stepped closer now, your boots crunching the gravel, I backed away. You stopped in place and your shoulders slackened.

"Looks like I caught you at a bad time," you said. "If you ever want to talk, pop on by. My family would love to have you and Aiden over for dinner. Especially Ellen. Think she's got a little crush on your boy."

I faked a cough. It hardly sounded convincing, but it was a last-ditch effort to explain my behavior.

"Appreciate it. Just not feeling well today," I said. "Think I caught a bug."

It was your turn to stare at the ground.

"Right," you said. You opened your mouth as if you had one more thing to say, but you shook your head and returned to your truck.

Couldn't see you leave through the dust you kicked up, but I watched anyway, my whole body shaking. My end was coming sooner than later.

***

There would've been easier ways to kill myself. Now I wish I'd tried them. I had a shotgun for turkey season and a rifle for coyotes who got too curious about my cattle. One pull of the trigger would've banished my pain and guilt forever. Instead, I asked Aiden to kill me.

After the bucking incident, I didn't bother taking him back to the stable. He roamed the pasture freely, but never stopped to eat or drink. I would know; I watched him plenty. It was only when he stared back that I busied myself with other work. See, his gaze scared me worse than his hooves.

But eventually I gathered the courage—or perhaps despair—to submit myself to him. It only seemed fair that he decide my fate.

It was late yesterday afternoon when I found him by the pasture's pond. Translucent tadpoles flitted through the crystal-clear water, and cattle drank deep, sloppy gulps. Aiden stood beside them, still as a sentry.

As I prepared my words, a ball welled up in my throat.

"I understand if you want me dead," I said. "If it gives you closure … if it helps you pass on, then I want that, too."

I got on my knees and inched closer to Aiden. My self-preservation instinct resisted the movement, but I forced myself to the ground. Face-down in itchy grass, I crawled toward Aiden's hooves. When I was an inch away, I drew in a shaky breath.

"Make it quick," I said. "Or draw it out, if that's what feels right. You might not believe it, but I just want you to find peace."

I could smell the musk of dirt and animal dander, the heavy stink of cow shit. I expected Aiden's hoof to crush my skull at any moment. My neck tensed and my lungs seized up. I squeezed my eyes shut and pictured Hell: a furnace-hot silo filled with churning, hungry grain. Death was seconds away, I was sure of it.

But nothing happened. Aiden didn't seem to notice my presence, or if he did, he didn't care to acknowledge it. I cried and whispered into the cracked earth.

"Please, Aiden. Please, just kill me."

I sobbed and pleaded and prodded his motionless hoof. Eventually, the grunting cattle finished drinking and roamed to the other side of the pasture. The blue sky succumbed to an orange wildfire haze. Death never came for me.

But you did. Screaming and praying, I didn't register your arrival. It wasn't until you grabbed my ankles and pulled me away from Aiden that I noticed. I swore and clawed at the ground, sharp grass slicing my palms. But when my panic subsided, I remembered the role I had to play.

"Darren," I said. "What are you doing here?"

"Figured I'd check in on you, man," you said. "Looks like that was the right call. You drunk or something? Heard you going on about all sorts of weird shit."

"What'd you hear?" The words slipped out before I could stop them. I sat up, dry grass balled in my bloody fists.

You towered over me like a silent god. Silhouetted against dusk, you glowed the color of rust, the color of blood.

"Where's Aiden, John?" you asked.

I fumbled for a response, but lying proved just as hard as living.

"I can't tell you," I said. A sob crept upward. Soon it would be impossible to contain.

"Alright, John," you said. Your words came out calm and even, like everything was either fine or going to be fine soon.

Maybe that's why I said what came out next: "Call the police, okay?"

You nodded and returned to your truck. I stayed in the pasture, sobbing.

Not long after, there were blue and red lights, handcuffs, and a thousand questions. I was still in the pasture when you and the cops found me, hugging Aiden's inert hoof like a teddy bear. I fessed up right away. Even told you about the horse. You might think I added that bit to bolster my insanity defense, but it's not like that. I just want someone to know what really became of Aiden. Someone to take care of him better than I ever could. If it's really him trapped inside that horse, trapped between worlds, I want him to know love one last time. I've seen how much you love your daughter, and I want you to love my son just the same. Is that too much to ask?

WHAT TO DO WITH GRANDPA

Excerpts from the notes of Kathy Garland, executor of the Lloyd Jennings estate

Interview with Lloyd Jennings

There's no need to recount my crimes, Miss Garland. You know them, my grandchildren know them, the pelicans and the groupers and the dolphins all know them. Most importantly, I know them—for now, at least. These days, my brain feels like a bowl of cornflakes left to soak, which is why I'll make my wishes clear while I'm still lucid.

Have you visited the levee lately? I asked my nurse—whose name escapes me—to take me there yesterday. I limped beside the crumbling structure, my feet throbbing and the poor man begging me to return to the care home van. He stopped begging when I slipped him a hundred—the least I could do—but his initial concern was not misplaced. I could've fallen, littered as the grounds were with drifters' ashen fire pits, fishermen's salt-crusted nets, and clay boulders shed from the levee like bolts from a speeding car. I stopped where the bulk of the detritus lay. That would be the spot. My final resting place.

You look at me like I'm mad. Like I should have the sense to be buried with my wife—God rest her soul—on that forested hill above the sea's present reach. But Laura, too, knew my crimes, so I wish to give her the gift of distance. I also wish to save this city when the hundred-year storm comes. Or rather, the storm my grandchildren will suffer every other year until the end of their lives. Thankfully, I've found a way to help them weather the terror. Perhaps even a way to save the world.

Listen carefully and write down exactly what I say, for these are God's words transmitted through dreams. Over the past year, His angels have visited me in my sleep, their wheels of eyes both judging and expectant. They have delivered one word of His command every night, burning each one indelibly into my otherwise deteriorating mind. It was only after the first hundred words that I understood their meaning—God's grand purpose for me.

Are you ready to hear it?

I am to be killed before hurricane season. If my rotting brain does not die naturally by then, you are to pull the trigger.

Don't interrupt. Keep listening. Keep writing.

After I'm dead, you are not to embalm me, cremate me, or donate my organs. You are to grind me into a fine paste. I am to become human concrete. Like a construction worker filling a pothole, you will place me in this most vulnerable section of the levee—the one I stopped at yesterday, marked here on this map. My concrete will harden. I will become one with the clay. And when the next storm comes, the levee will hold. My grandchildren will survive. Your grandchildren will survive.

You want that, right?

Then obey God's command.

***

Interview with Helen Jennings

I'm glad you came to me first. You're probably planning to talk with Kai and J.P., too, but trust me: I'm the only sane grandchild. Kai spends too much time on communist Twitter, and J.P. thinks crystals will cure their IBS. Sorry if that's TMI, but you have to understand what my siblings are like. Neither of them has Grandpa's best interests at heart.

I'm the only one who thinks of him as human. And sure, he fucked up, but just like any other human, he can change. I know what Kai would say right now: "What, Helen, you're going to forgive Grandpa for causing the apocalypse just because he *feels bad*?" Yes, I am, you cynical asshole. Grandpa knows he can't fix this nightmare, but at least he's *trying* in his own weird way. Most people in his position would have fucked off to one of their ten climate-proofed mansions or luxury bunkers until the end of their days. Not Grandpa.

I'll admit, I have a soft spot for him. My first memory was holding his hand—I was four at the time—and walking down Carnival Pier. That place sank into the ocean ten years back, but it was pure childhood magic while it lasted, blessed with the greasy sweetness of funnel cake fumes, a Ferris wheel perched over sparkling sunset waters, and plenty of stuffed animal prize games. That day, Grandpa led me to the balloon dart stand and promised to reveal a secret if I could pop at least two balloons. I only got one, but I begged him to tell me anyway. He shook his head, but from how he smiled, he would've told no matter what—even if my darts had hit the carnival worker. He bent down on one knee and told me I was going to be a big sister. It started raining right then, so we wouldn't be able to do bumper cars, but I didn't care. I jumped and squealed and hugged his legs as if he'd delivered both the news and the baby that very moment.

How could I hate someone who gave me such a beautiful first memory? Sure, when Kai was born, he didn't live up to expectations, but Grandpa couldn't have predicted that. If Kai were here right now, he'd find a way to ruin what I just told you. He'd say something about Grandpa rushing me home from Carnival Pier so he could squeeze in a few more hours sludging up the Gulf of Mexico. Kai can fuck off. Here, take this picture for instance. I look at myself sitting on Grandpa's knee, both of us smiling, and see two happy people. Kai looks at the same picture and all he can think of is the burning world just outside the frame. What a joyless perspective.

Jeez, what am I doing? You're not a family therapist. Let's get back on track. You were asking about what to do with Grandpa.

His human concrete idea is … well, it's unhinged. Unethical. Not to mention impossible—a person can't just become concrete. But most importantly, it's proof of how poorly his dementia treatment is going. He's reluctant to spend his "blood money"— funny thing, Kai calls it that too; might be the only thing he and Grandpa agree on—but he should use it to pay for higher quality memory care. I've found some facilities nearby. Well, a couple hundred miles off, but close enough. Look at this one. A hundred five-star reviews. Nice, right? We could send him there. Better treatment might get that human concrete idea out of his head. He'd be able to enjoy the end of his life and remember the good old days.

That's all I want. To reminisce with him about Carnival Pier and see him smile again. Last time I mentioned the place, he grunted, looked down at his mashed potatoes, and said, "Atlantis, you mean. The mermen took it. I sold it to them." All I could do was sigh.

But enough of my rambling. Let's spend some money and get his mind right. If Kai disagrees, he can eat shit.

***

Interview with Kai Jennings

If you're expecting me to agree with anything Helen says, I'll stop you right there. Yes, she's my older sister, but she's also an idiot who thinks recycling a spinach container will stop the twelfth reincarnation of Hurricane Katrina. The kind of dipshit who— what? Yeah, sure, I'll get on with it.

Let me tell you, it's fucking weird organizing with communists who know about my grandpa. Most of them don't hold it against me since they've got complicated family shit, too: Lila with her Republican governor uncle and Mark with that trust fund his mom won't let him touch until he "grows the hell up."

Gotta say, when you emailed me about Grandpa's idea, I was thrilled. Figured, hell, let him take the bullet. Let him become pink McNugget paste and join the levee. But when I told my friends about the plan, they proposed something else. I'm all about it, but you'll probably hate it.

Shit, you're sweating. Want a beer? I've got some in the—no? Cool, cool.

It's funny. Grandpa and I have never agreed on a single goddamn thing, but now we have some common ground. I've wanted him to die for years, and he's finally on board with the idea. But he shouldn't decide how it happens. Think about it. Would you let a Nazi pick their own execution method? *Bitte, make it painless. Let me pass in the loving presence of meine Frau und Kinder.* Hell no.

Here's what my friends came up with. First off, Grandpa can't be allowed to redeem himself. No becoming human concrete to "save the levee." None of that puke-inducing savior complex bullshit. Second—and this seems obvious—but he needs to suffer. Death by a thousand cuts. We'll tie the bastard up and let everyone in town take a slash at him. BYO knife, you know what I mean?

My partner Dallas would be more than happy to spill some blood. Last year's floods killed his mom. Kathleen had mobility issues and couldn't get out of her basement apartment before it flooded. Fucking tragic. Dallas and I used to go over there every Sunday to play poker with her. Woman had a mean poker face and could talk shit like nobody's business. Damn, she was rad.

So, yeah, I'm cool with Dallas dragging a razor across Grandpa's chest. Might make him bleed out before everyone else has their turn, but it'll be just the therapy Dallas needs. Hell, even if everyone else just watches, it'll be damn cathartic.

Huh? No, I'm not saying this shit will save us. Nothing short of systemic collapse will save us. Until then, you're just as doomed as I am. Shit, you'd probably benefit from communal bloodletting, too. How would you like to shove that fountain pen in my grandpa's gut?

***

Interview with J.P. Jennings

You look tired. Don't take that the wrong way. Can I offer you tea? I can't get the good stuff anymore—supply chain collapse and all—but there's nothing wrong with your basic green. No? That's perfectly fine. I'm sure you've had a long day, especially visiting Kai and Helen. They're, well … you know.

Let me guess. Kai wants to publicly execute Grandpa and Helen wants to boost his dementia treatment? Yep, sounds like my siblings. They're both sort of right. Kai at least has an appreciation for the power of ritual, and Helen makes up for what Kai lacks in the human dignity department. But why not get the best of both worlds?

You seem lost. I'll explain.

See, everyone's assuming Grandpa's gone insane. Yes, he has dementia, and yes, he served me a cup of hand soap as a drink last time I visited him, but he's not *always* off his rocker. His human concrete idea, for instance. My siblings think it's a delusion. I think— and stick with me here—I think it's a *vision*. Could be from God, Yahweh, Allah, Vishnu, Gaia. Whoever. But *Someone* is giving him another chance. Giving *humanity* another chance. Become the levee. Redeem yourself. Save the world and all its beautiful creatures.

I've seen that look before, mostly from Kai, but I'm used to it. Guess I've always been the patchouli-smelling black sheep of the family. Too sincere, too *woo*. Take any Sunday morning growing up: Helen doing homework, Kai playing first-person shooters, and me begging them for a ride to church, temple, mosque—anywhere with a spiritual connection. Helen always asked why I wasted time with something so boring, and Kai always yelled at me for interrupting his game. Neither gave me a ride.

Grandpa was the only person who agreed to it. Given his work and golf schedule, it didn't happen often, but when it did, I felt radiant with both his love and the Divine's. The last time he took me to a service, I was thirteen. I asked if we could go to the Buddhist temple. He laughed, but it wasn't a mocking laugh—more a "you surprise me every day, kid" laugh. Used to the pews and kneelers of his Catholic days, he was surprised to learn we'd be sitting on the floor for the service. Still, he went along with it. He even participated in the prayers and chants to the best of his ability.

Naively, I mistook his participation for buy-in, but when the service ended, he said, "Can't say this worship stuff is for me, but if you liked it, I can take you again after my Houston trip."

His comment both warmed and broke my heart. He loved me more than my siblings did—that much was clear—but he'd never be a spiritual seeker. I stopped inviting him to services after that, but he never brought it up.

You can probably guess how I felt, over a decade later, when he told me God had a plan for him. It was the first time I'd felt genuine hope in ages. Can you blame me though? I've only been alive for twenty-five years, and I've seen water swallow whole neighborhoods and fire devour whole forests. I've seen cornfields shrivel and orchards rot. I've seen clusters of monarchs grow thinner each year and firefly light shows fizzle to nothing and—

Yes, thank you. A tissue would be nice. I just … I get swept away sometimes. It's hard, these changes. To see Mother Nature dying and feel myself dying with Her.

But please. I'm begging you. Let Grandpa fulfill his vision. We can't afford to drown again.

***

Notes from Kathy Garland

After weeks of negotiation, the Jennings family came to a compromise that left no one satisfied. When we carried out the plan, Helen fled the scene in tears, Kai called it "another bullshit half measure," and J.P. prayed their grandfather's lessened sacrifice would be enough.

On that day, I picked up Mr. Jennings from his care home and drove him to the surgical hospital. When we arrived, his grandchildren were waiting in the lobby, seated far away from each other, and not speaking. Mr. Jennings hobbled over to J.P. and Helen for a hug but skipped Kai.

A moment later the surgeon entered with a sour expression.

"I'm scheduled to perform a heart surgery at eleven," she said. "Can we get this started?"

Mr. Jennings nodded. "Of course, Miss … "

"Doctor. Doctor Lund."

The surgeon never would have agreed to perform this elective amputation were it not for the legal agreement and $100,000 cash payment—a meager sum as far as Mr. Jennings's finances are concerned, but enough for Dr. Lund.

We followed her into the operating room. She drew a curtain across the surgical table as if she didn't want passing colleagues to see her performing the bizarre operation. She couldn't do much about soundproofing, though. The terms of our agreement stated that Mr. Jennings was not to receive anesthetic during the leg amputations, per Kai's request.

As soon as Dr. Lund gathered her tools, she asked Mr. Jennings if he was ready, but the real question lingering in her eyes was "are you insane?" Mr. Jennings only nodded. The grandchildren had the opportunity to leave, but none of them budged.

Dr. Lund operated immediately, as if any hesitation would cause her to flee the room and forfeit her payment. Blood sprayed everywhere: her surgical gown, the white curtain, and Helen's screaming mouth. The distressed grandchild ran out the door and never came back. I called her later that morning out of courtesy, but she didn't pick up.

Throughout the procedure, Mr. Jennings almost never screamed. Mostly he gasped and moaned and chanted "I am the concrete that binds, I am the wall that protects, I am the shield of the Lord." He was pale as the hospital walls when his second leg flopped into the sanitized metal tray. Dr. Lund quickly stapled the stumps and cleaned the blood.

J.P. pulled a glass dropper bottle from their fringe purse. It contained some sort of oil, which they anointed the legs with before placing them in a cloth sack. Dr. Lund noticed and muttered, "Jesus Christ."

After the final staple sealed his left stump, Mr. Jennings smiled. Kai sighed, let out a string of curses, and stomped out the room.

Dr. Lund's arms trembled when she addressed her patient: "Okay, Mr. Jennings. A nurse will bring you to your bed shortly. Recovery is normally three to seven days but given your age and the fact that you requested both legs be removed, it might be longer. We can't legally deny you pain management medication, but I understand you have some sort of … agreement with your family. Do what's best for you. Are there any questions or …?"

She was already halfway out the door, as if she couldn't be delayed a second longer. Mr. Jennings mumbled a "thank you" and a "you're welcome". Dr. Lund frowned, shook her head, and then rushed off to her next surgery.

Still lying on the surgical table, Mr. Jennings turned toward J.P. His voice came out breathy and gentle: "You have everything you need. I trust you'll do what's necessary before … well, I'm not sure what will happen. Only God knows. But something's coming and we don't have much time."

"I know, Grandpa." J.P. grabbed his hands and sniffled. "I feel it, too."

Tears welled in J.P.'s eyes, then in Mr. Jennings's. Even I felt the hot prick of emotion.

The moment dissolved when a nurse pushing a wheelchair creaked the door open. He eyed the gore-soaked sack at J.P.'s feet, then put on a strained smile for Mr. Jennings.

"Ready?" he said.

Mr. Jennings pecked J.P. on the cheek, closed his eyes, and muttered his agreement. It took a few minutes of pained moans to load him onto the wheelchair. Then he and the nurse were gone.

AC pumped into the room at a dull roar, circulating coppery air. A custodian would be here soon. I looked down at the leaking bag, then up at J.P.

"Meet you at the woodchipper?" I asked.

"And then the levee," they replied.

Then off we went to save humankind.

A Creature Nailed Upon the Corridor of Time

<u>The Journal of Dr. Molly Welch: June 23rd, 2024, [LOCATION REDACTED]</u>

Orla keeps telling me how good this discovery will be for my career, and I keep telling her how good it will be for science. She's not wrong though. Unearthing a fossil like this one would propel any paleontologist's career to the moon. That said, I've always shied away from the limelight and there are no (known) fossils on the moon. I'm here to better understand Earth's natural history and unravel the mysteries this lonesome rock has to offer.

And what a mystery this fossil is. The head and beak alone are the length of a semi truck and perfectly preserved. Scarlet feathers cover the face save for a golden circle around the closed eye. (How I'd love to peel that eye open and see if it's just as well preserved ...) The hooked beak is also golden and viciously serrated.

My team has yet to uncover the rest of the fossil, but if its head is any indication of its body's size, this dig will likely take months. Not that I'm complaining. This is what I've dreamed of ever since I was a child, scooping sand at the beach, not to build castles, but to find megalodon teeth. Even as a lifelong dreamer, I never imagined I'd be the one to find such a historic discovery.

Not a single expert I've spoken with can identify this specimen. It's the first of its kind ever found in the fossil record. And what's even stranger is that we discovered it in the Albion Formation, which is only 120,000 years old. To think that humans existed at the same time as this creature is hard to fathom.

I have countless more questions, but one has been bugging me in particular. How could this specimen have been preserved so perfectly, feathers and all? True-form preservation only ever happens if an organism has been trapped in amber, desiccated, or frozen. None of those conditions seem to apply here. Yet another mystery to unravel. Perhaps we'll find more answers soon.

The Journal of Dr. Molly Welch: June 29th, 2024

I'm not sure I can take another shock. The surprises have hit me one after another this week, and it's been hard to sleep. So here I am, at three in the morning, typing away at my laptop with the backlight turned all the way down. Orla is trying to sleep behind me. I'll come to bed and hold her once I'm done. Admittedly, I've not been the most attentive partner lately. I'm sure Orla understands with everything going on, but that pained look in her eyes tells me she needs more than I'm giving. I swear I'll do better after work on the dig slows down.

Speaking of the dig, I can hardly believe what we found today: an indication that humans killed the Titan (our working name for the specimen). At the base of its neck, we discovered seven carved granite stakes pinning the creature to the ground. It's incredible to think ancient humans successfully hunted this creature, but what's odd is that there's no indication of the creature being stripped for meat or other resources. Was it hunted for sport? Killed ritualistically? So many mysteries that might forever remain as such.

There's no chance I'll sleep tonight. Sorry, Orla.

<u>The Journal of Dr. Molly Welch: June 30th, 2024</u>

The Titan's eye was open when we arrived at the dig site. Everyone thought I was responsible because I kept going on about wanting to see it, but no, I would never attempt something so reckless on such a perfect fossil.

We still haven't figured out who did it, but what does it matter? The eye is open. It's unlike any I've ever seen. I don't know how else to describe it other than Vantablack. You know, that lab-created shade that consumes 99.965% of all light? We checked to make sure it wasn't a vacant socket shrouded in shadow, but it most certainly contained an eye—the organ itself—miraculously preserved. I've never seen a purer darkness. It was easy to get lost in it. I stood there transfixed for what felt like only a moment but was actually an hour, according to my watch.

You'd think the eye would've made the day's dig a joyous occasion despite the August heat, but the crew barely spoke after that. Most took an extra-long lunch, as if returning to the Titan were a dreaded task. I tried to reignite some enthusiasm by joking around and sharing Orla's homemade lemon bars, but even I had to admit I wasn't quite feeling up for it. The eye unnerved me, and even if it hadn't seen a thing for 120,000 years, I still didn't like the ridiculous feeling of being watched.

Thankfully, just as some anonymous culprit had opened the eye, some anonymous saint covered it with a tarp. Work continued after that, though the pace was still slow and the crew was still quiet. My mood matched everyone else's, troubled by the presence of a sneaky liar whose recklessness could jeopardize the dig.

Perhaps tomorrow will bring answers and joy. I can only hope.

<u>The Journal of Dr. Molly Welch: July 4th, 2024</u>

Orla is furious that I'm not spending the holiday with her. I joked that the Fourth was a celebration for Smokey the Bear haters, and she stormed out of the room after that. She's right, though. I should be at home with her doing moisturizing face masks, watching nature documentaries, and comforting our firework-traumatized dog.

But I've been working on a secret project. Orla initially thought it was for her—went as far as calling her mom and telling her she suspected I was going to propose—but I threw water on that notion quickly—and perhaps tactlessly. The look on her face when I told her the secret project was for the crew … well, it was like a death laser aimed straight between my eyes. What she doesn't understand is how important this project is. The crew has been in low spirits. Too many of us have been sleeping poorly, stumbling through the work day, and calling in sick. I get it. This dig is more intense than any other I've done. Between all the press coverage, paperwork, and coordination between scientific, historical, and governmental agencies, it makes sense that we'd be tired. That, and the eye. Every morning, we arrive to find the tarp covering the eye has vanished. Even when we pin it down with rocks, it disappears. I'm sure it's just someone messing with us, but the effect on the crew's morale has been undeniable. Good thing I have the perfect pick-me-up—or *will* have the perfect pick-me-up if everything goes to plan.

To get what I needed, I visited the dig site alone today. The location is secured now—government agents and all—but the guards recognized me and let me in. The fenced-in area is the size of a football stadium, which I rather appreciate. Imagine how lovely the world would be if all football stadiums were converted into paleontological dig sites.

Daydreaming aside, it was the strangeness of what I found on the Titan that troubled me. I was unloading equipment for my project when I noticed something at the corner of the creature's eye: wet, yellow clumps. I set down the equipment to get a closer look. The substance didn't appear to be either a fungus or feces from some passerby bird. The cornea also appeared to be intact, all of its innards still encased. Whatever it was looked like eye gunk

—the kind Orla rubbed off of me each morning as if she were a chimp grooming her mate. I laughed at the impossibility. I would've taken a sample of the gunk, but the prospect of finding an answer made me nervous.

Ultimately, the substance's origins didn't matter so much as what I'd come to do. I spent several hours getting scans of the Titan. I hesitate to describe my project further in case it fails, but if it works out, you best believe I'll journal about it.

That's all for now though. I'm writing this from the couch where I'll sleep tonight. Orla locked the bedroom door and left the dog out here for me to take care of in case a firework scares her. I know I'm deep in the shit, but if this project ends up being as spectacular as I imagine it'll be, Orla will understand and invite me back to bed. I just know it.

The Journal of Dr. Molly Welch: July 10th, 2024

We thought the rest of the fossil was missing, but its body parts had long ago been severed and scattered. Whoever killed the Titan— a task that must have taken a few dozen humans—cut off its limbs, moved them far apart from each other, and pinned them to the ground with seven stakes, same as the head. The killing seems ritualistic, like a sacrifice to gain some ancient god's favor. I'm out of my depth here—just a humble paleontologist with a wild imagination—but my gut tells me I'm right. And my gut won't stop twisting at the sinister possibilities …

Of course, I'm still helping with the dig, but I've also been staying up late to finish this secret project. It's done now, so I feel comfortable writing about it now. You ready? (By "you," I suppose I mean future me, reminiscing in twenty years' time.) Okay, here it is: I'm recreating the Titan's vocalizations. When I visited the dig site on the Fourth, I scanned the creature's throat, chest, and larynx. Given the weight my name carries in the paleontology world right now, the university was more than happy to lend me the necessary equipment, though it could scarcely be called standard use in my field. They also lent me the software needed for simulating the vocalizations—a high-tech program capable of rendering such simulations within minutes. Funny thing is, the vocal simulation took *days* to render. I mean, yes, what's a few days, geologically speaking? But I have to wonder why it took so long. Are the Titan's vocalization organs far more complex than any other this software has encountered? After what Orla and I heard, I'm inclined to think so.

Speaking of Orla, she established a rule that, if I don't join her in bed before midnight, she locks the door. Well, big surprise, she locked the door this evening. I finished the render around 3 a.m., so I had to knock to wake her. I could deal with it if she made me sleep on the couch again, but I would've been heartbroken if she refused to listen to the vocal simulation with me. It was important we were together for the first time it played. Thankfully, after some grumbling and a few choice words, Orla unlocked the bedroom door and came into my office. There was gunk in the corners of her eyes that looked identical to what I'd found in the Titan's eye. The similarity made me shudder, so I reached out to rub it away. Orla flinched back, squinted, and told me not to touch her. That hurt, I admit, but I could take her pissiness as long as she reacted positively to the big reveal. If I'd known how she'd *actually* react, I would've let her keep sleeping.

Here's how it happened. She sat on the office carpet, rested her chin in her palm, and asked how long this would take. I assured her it would only be a minute, then allowed a brief dramatic pause. Apparently, it wasn't brief enough because Orla snapped at me to get it over with. That hurt a bit, too, but I figured her grumpiness would transform into excitement as soon as I pressed "play." I hit the button.

The low, dissonant roar that emerged was simultaneously animal and alien. While the volume wasn't all that high, the speaker crackled and smoked after just a few seconds. It was as if the device wasn't equipped to handle a sound that hadn't existed for thousands of years. The audio warped into a hideous hiss, but it was hard to say if that came from the vocal simulation or the busted speaker. Every hair on my body bristled. Orla screamed, fell to her knees, and scrambled backward out of the room. I wanted to follow her and calm her down, but all I could do was stand there until the speaker shat the bed completely a minute later. The room smelled acrid, like burning electronics. I remained motionless, and even though the audio had stopped, my hair still stood on end. The bedroom door lock clicked. Safe behind it, Orla sobbed.

When I collected myself as much as possible, I stood outside that door, trying to reassure Orla that everything was fine. My voice sounded choked and raspy. Orla's sobs died down to the occasional hiccup but never to a snore.

By now, too late at night has turned into too early in the morning, and we're both up in our separate spaces. Something tells me our relationship is reaching a tipping point. Maybe I should call into work tomorrow (or today, as it's 5 a.m.) and spend the day with Orla. A rescheduled Fourth of July, minus the gross patriotism and environmental devastation.

But the vocal simulation … I promised the crew I'd share it with them. I didn't tell them what it was, of course, but some of them looked excited. I can't break a promise. I'll go into work and show them the sound that hasn't yet left my head. My heart is still pounding and feels like nothing—not deep breaths, not meditation, not medication—can slow it down. No way I'll sleep. Might as well get an early start.

The Journal of Dr. Molly Welch: July 11th, 2024

I don't know if I'll ever stop shaking. It's all my fault. I found the Titan, I created the vocal simulation, I played it at the dig site for everyone to hear.

Hell broke loose at lunchtime. The crew gathered under a tent to avoid the noontime sun, waves of heat snaking upward like desert ghosts. We sat at white picnic tables, eating catered sub sandwiches left sitting an hour too long. While lunch had once been a time of laughter and conversation, our cumulative exhaustion had snuffed out this enthusiasm. Only the sound of chewing and the ruffle of windblown tent flaps remained.

I broke the silence by standing and clearing my throat. Lucky (or rather, *unlucky*) me, last night's speaker wasn't the only one I owned. I held up a different one, newer and higher quality, less likely to break when the audio played. At first, the crew looked at me like I'd interrupted a funeral, but when I reminded them of the secret project reveal, some of the tension melted away. A few smiled and put their sandwiches down while others whispered to their colleagues, speculating on the nature of this reveal. Only one or two crew members seemed genuinely apprehensive. I hoped they wouldn't react as Orla had.

Of course, I'd prepared a speech, but I'd forgotten its most dramatic moments in my sleep-deprived state. Still, the promise of hearing the Titan's call was enough to get folks shutting up and leaning in. I grinned, then hesitated before pressing the button. As stupid as it sounds, part of me was afraid to hear the audio again. I wasn't afraid of the speaker busting or the crew expressing disappointment. No, the audio itself scared me. I glanced toward the Titan, not a hundred feet from the tent, its gunked-up void of an eye dead but watching. Watching me. I shivered and turned toward the crew once more. Some of their smiles strained as if they'd been held too long and left unfulfilled in their anticipation. I couldn't keep them waiting. I dismissed my reservations and pressed "play."

The Titan's simulated call burst like water from a broken dam. I expected I'd have a less intense reaction, having already heard the sound once, but no. Every muscle in my body tightened, as if my flesh were crystalizing, becoming simultaneously rocklike and easy to shatter. Even if I could've escaped my paralysis and silenced the speaker, it wouldn't have done any good. The damage was done within seconds.

Two crew members fainted. One vomited on the table. Another scrambled to free herself from the picnic table only to get her leg stuck in the metal frame. She screamed as if the table were trapping her in an early grave.

And then there was the earthquake. No fault lines were nearby, but what else could it have been? The ground shook with astonishing violence. The tent collapsed on top of us, a suffocating sea of hot white polyethylene. None of us could escape as we screamed and thrashed against the material and felt pebbles hop beneath our quaking feet. The vocal simulation kept playing, but the origin of the noise seemed to shift, as if played on a surround sound system with one side much louder than the other. Whether the speaker echoed against the fallen fabric or the matching sound source came from outside the tent ... no, I won't accept the latter as a possibility. I can't. It's outlandish, impossible. But how can I deny the impossible when it has engulfed me for the duration of this dig?

The earthquake—if that's what it was—ended as soon as it began. My speaker died, too, its mesh blown to pieces and melting. I unburied myself from the tent and helped the rest of the crew out. Some were unconscious and wouldn't wake up. The awake ones were catatonic, wide-eyed and shaking with blood leaking out of their ears. The woman who got her leg stuck had a broken shin and wouldn't stop sobbing. I was in the best shape of anyone, but that wasn't saying much. I stood on wobbly feet, barely able to keep my balance.

When one of the government agents ran over to ask if I was okay, I could answer only in clipped phrases. *We're fine*, I lied. *Just an earthquake.* It felt wrong to omit the vocal simulation from my account, as if the two were somehow related to the earthquake, but I stopped myself from mentioning it. The implication bordered on insanity.

Before the agent left, I asked what he'd seen from outside the tent. He blinked hard as if the thought hadn't occurred to him, and then a blankness washed over his gaze.

"There was a dust cloud around the dig site and then…" The man paused, cracked a weak smile, and shook his head. "And then it settled, I suppose."

I want to believe him. I wish I did.

And now I'm at home, shaking like a dog left out in the rain. I wish Orla would unlock that door, forget my transgressions of the past few weeks, and hold me. God, how I want to be held.

The Journal of Dr. Molly Welch: July 12th, 2024

I showed up at the dig site hungover. I'd planned on staying home with Orla, but she left a note saying … well, I won't get into it. That wound is still too fresh.

In any case, the rest of the crew called in sick. Well, most didn't call in at all. But if ever there was a time to forgive a "no call no show," it's now. I get it. I really do. And I wouldn't blame them if they never came back.

As for me, what else do I have left but the Titan? Most of her anyway. Her right wing is missing. When I arrived this morning, the government agents were gathered around where her wing used to be. Some had badges for agencies I'd never even heard of and others carried guns that looked capable of striking down the moon. I tried to push through them. I wanted to witness the absence, make sense of it. I wanted to find a crevice or sinkhole the wing could've slipped into, but instead there was solid rock in the shape of her. Though a guard blocked my view, I could make out the stone stakes, still present but snapped in half. I overheard agents discussing theories. Perhaps a first earthquake had opened a crack in the earth that swallowed the wing and a second earthquake had closed the crack back up. Or maybe thieves had stolen the wing in the night. The absurdity of these theories made me laugh, but not in amusement. The highest-ranking, best-equipped, and ostensibly most knowledgeable members of our government were stumped. Sure, they'll eventually come up with an official explanation, but only to project the illusion of control and understanding. Reality is boiling water trickling between our fingers. The more we try to capture it, the more it burns us. We'll never be able to cradle it in our palms and gaze into its liquid truth. Its escape is inevitable.

Not long after I arrived at the dig site, two men escorted me away. Apparently, my laughter had become uncontrollable and was disturbing the investigators. It was no longer the place for an archeologist anyway. I don't imagine I'll ever return. But who knows? I might see the Titan again, her single wing flapping soundlessly across the night sky, blacking out the moon and stars in search of her missing body. I pray she never finds it.

The Strangling Ash

Uncle Halvar pours Father's ashes into the vision chamber and smacks the urn to shake loose the rest of him. He closes the chamber's glass top before descending the ladder, the solstice sun beating down on him. Dirt darkens his face and tears darken the dirt, but he doesn't make a show of his suffering; he must tend to his ceremonial duties.

"Come." He gestures for Grandmother Yrsa, Aunt Sigrid, and me to enter the forest clearing. Uncle's hands are red and wrinkled as dried apples from years of working the forge. Those hands built the armor Father died in, plate too thin to stop the Christian invader's spear.

"Mother, the chamber invites you," Uncle says.

Chin quivering, Grandmother steps inside. The tall stone cylinder is the width of a well and looks cramped from the outside, but looks can be deceiving. Father taught me that with his smile—those charming pearls concealing his dragon fire. Uncle shuts the heavy door behind Grandmother, then pumps the bellows with his foot. Though I can't see it, I know that the air bursts into the chamber with enough force to swirl Father's ashes. A vision will form in the gale of gray—Father's final message to Grandmother before he passes on. I won't see the vision intended for me until after Grandmother and Aunt Sigrid go—elders first, always.

They knew Father when he was a boy of my age. I wonder if he was different then, if he skipped rocks and laughed and sang the Old Gods' songs. Or maybe, like me, he dreamed of escaping the human world to join the elves in their hidden forest kingdoms. Maybe he also had a father who hid his dragon fire in polite company, not so much as a tendril of smoke leaking from the corner of his mouth. I never met Grandfather or asked what he was like. Asking Father a question had always been a gamble, half the time ending in a curt response and the other half ending with a stinging cheek.

The chamber door sticks. Uncle grunts as he pries it open. Grandmother emerges laughing and covered in ash. Happy tears streak her face.

Uncle turns to Aunt: "Sigrid, the chamber invites you."

Aunt enters. Uncle closes the door behind her, stone grinding against stone until she's sealed in.

Grandmother hobbles in my direction, then leans down to whisper: "His swirling ashes smiled at me. A force for joy even in death. That's your father, through and through."

Uncle nods. "A ceaseless light in the dark."

Grandmother rubs my back with her bony hand, a gesture intended to comfort that only emphasizes the gulf between us. What does she know of her own son? Of the man, bearded and grown and tyrant of his hovel? I called him Father. He called me Mother Killer, as if I were to blame for the complications of my birth. Were it not for Grandmother, I might never have known my name.

But it's too late to reveal this darkness. Reputations of the dead are like mountain glaciers: permanent, unconquerable.

The door resists but eventually yields to Uncle's sweat and muscle. Aunt Sigrid stumbles out. Even through the gray, her cheeks burn a livid red.

"His ashes formed the face of the Christian who killed him," she says. "A face I could recognize in a crowd. We'll have our vengeance."

Her body quakes. Flecks of spit spray through her gritted teeth. Uncle abandons the bellows and embraces her.

His whisper breathes both gentleness and violence: "We'll thrust his head on a spike. Ravens will pick the bastard clean."

When Aunt stops shaking, Uncle returns to the chamber, foot poised above the bellows.

"Arne." We lock eyes. "The chamber invites you."

My feet itch, eager to flee into the woods, the mountains, even the Christian land—anywhere but the chamber. Whatever vision awaits me changes nothing. I still throb with the bruises of Father's final days, as if his anger were an ember, seething with heat even as its glow faded.

"Don't be afraid." Grandmother again places her hand on my back.

Her fingers feel like ice. I jerk forward. She'll keep touching me until I face the inevitable. I take a deep breath. Then another. And then it's into the chamber.

Uncle closes the door.

Looks didn't deceive me this time; the blackened stone walls hug me, prickly with the dust of a thousand dead. Dust from before Father, before Grandfather, and long, long before the Christian invaders.

A shaft of sunlight penetrates the cloudy glass roof. Bits of Father's ash float through the chamber and cling to me like spider's web, but most of him has settled on the floor. A gray dune on a ghostly beach. I resist the urge to kick it away.

A blast of air makes me jump. Uncle's pumping the bellows. Ash rises, tickles its way up my legs, swirls around me like wolves circling prey. It reaches my waist, chest, neck, consuming more of me in its ever-quickening storm. I accidentally breathe it in—dry, unbearably hot—and choke. I cough and gasp and find no relief. Father's vision be damned, I close my eyes and sink to the floor in hopes of locating a pocket of fresh air. But the dust is hotter and thicker down here. I retch, bile slicking my chin. The swirl of ash grows denser.

Maybe Father has no final vision for me. No wisdom to carry into my future. No call for joy or vengeance or endurance. Maybe the pain is the point. The strangling ash, his last chance to torment me. He'll take me with him if he can.

I jam my shoulder into the stone door and discover it unyielding as the mountain glacier, fixed as Father's memory in my family's eyes. I'm trapped in here with a joyful man, a brave warrior, a wronged widower. I scream. And as the bellows wheeze and the wind churns, I swear his ashes are laughing.

FLOATERS

(First published by *Hyphen-Punk*)

I watch him clock in at the quarry office and immediately know he'll be a floater. It's that puffiness in his cheeks, too pronounced to come from some late-night bender. I could shoot him right there in reception just to get the hideous act over with, but the law calls that murder. It's not until people are skyborne that I'm allowed to pull the trigger, so I'll have to keep an eye on this guy all day.

The last time I let a floater get away—some quarry manager drifting up past the clouds to God knows where, my harpoon missing him—Mr. Laurent warned me not to fuck up again. If I didn't need the money, I would've loved for him to fire me right then, his French accent thick with disappointment: "Miz Torres, I am afraid you muszt turn in your badge and gun. You are releaszed from duty." But I can tell by his frequent not-so-subtle glances down my blouse that he'd forgive a second mistake, probably a third, without issuing a pink slip. Most workers at the quarry are men with greasy faces and balding heads. The only other woman who worked here was Mr. Laurent's secretary, but she floated two days back. I shot her down myself—harpooned her in the gut and used the rope to reel her back to Earth. Mr. Laurent wept, probably because he was in love with her, his wife at home be damned. At least the life insurance check soothed his pain. See, he takes out policies for all of his employees, but the only way he can collect is if there's a body to prove they actually died. Every floater I down is another $50K in his pocket, and if that isn't a reason to keep me on the payroll, I don't know what is.

Can't lie, though, I've been drinking a lot more since I started this job six months ago. I know the government says people are dead the second they float, but the ones I down still haunt my dreams. I see their faces puffed up like balloons, their eyes bulging like deep-sea fish suffering from the bends. Even after the floaters have deflated, my tinnitus continues its steady hiss in the background, a constant reminder of what I've done.

My dad says I'm doing the floaters a favor by putting them out of their misery. "Just like putting a sick dog to sleep." He works at a veterinary clinic and has never been a people person, so how he thinks is no surprise. There's some truth to it, though. Scientists say all floaters have one thing in common: deteriorating mental health in the months leading up to their ascension. Ten years ago, before anyone started floating, those same folks might've put a gun in their mouth or swallowed too many pills. Still, the numbers are off; there are way more floaters today than suicides a decade back.

I digress. Going down these rabbit holes is easy when you're a harpooner. My job is an awful lot like being in the military: boredom ninety percent of the time and fast-paced, traumatizing violence the other ten. Here I am now, standing in the limestone quarry, slogging my way through that ninety percent. My skin is the darkest it's ever been in this blistering sun, and the clatter of metal against rock aggravates my tinnitus. My feet ache from standing so long, even though I should be used to the pain by now. I've kept my eye on the future floater for the past four hours, but if I'm being honest, my focus has been on my wristwatch. Four hours until I can go home and drink on the couch. Eight hours until I can have nightmares again. Haven't had a night without them in six months.

A loud bell signals lunch time. The workers shut down their machines, wipe their sweaty brows, and hustle to the cafeteria. It's my job to watch the men while they eat, my harpoon gun at the ready in case the puffy guy floats away from the table. Luckily, that hasn't happened yet. I can only imagine how the men would scream seeing me harpoon their bloated co-worker to death while blood sprays all over their sack lunches.

I follow the crew toward the cafeteria but take my sweet time. They file in without me, and it's nice being left outside in relative silence: no grinding machinery, no trucks beeping as they reverse, and no men howling at Mr. Laurent's misogynistic jokes. I'd rather hear my tinnitus than that shit any day. Instead of going inside, I take another lap around the building. It'll give the crew some time to enjoy their meals without the chilling presence of a harpooner. I might be neglecting my duties, but there's no denying I'm considerate.

Rocks crunch under my boots as I circle the building. I unhook the pocket knife from my belt and twirl it to entertain myself. Overhead, clouds have covered the sun, and the first cool breeze in hours blows through my hair. I close my eyes and soak in the feeling. It's rare I get a moment like this on the job—nature's little joys intruding on this diesel-smelling, scarred-up quarry. I smile for the first time in months.

My smile fades when Mr. Laurent calls from his personal office building a football field away. My brief moment of peace ruined, illusory.

"Miz Torres," he cries. "Why are you just standing around?"

I sigh and wave my hand in lieu of an apology. I can't bear to say sorry to the man. Not anymore.

But when I start toward the cafeteria door, something is off. My feet don't crunch the gravel. They make no sound at all. Each step gets me nowhere. Something pinches the back of my neck like a cat lifting its kitten by the scruff. That tight, painful feeling spreads to my cheeks, arms, and gut. I look down. I'm floating. My body climbs a few inches higher every second.

When I'm eye-level with the building's roof, I grip the gutter, as if clinging to Earth has ever kept any floater from drifting skyward. A forceful pull peels my fingers loose, and I'm no longer rooted. I keep floating. This is it. My life over before I could make anything of it.

Mr. Laurent screams, "Miz Torres, Miz Torres! Use the gun. Please, use it!"

The harpoon gun is strapped to my shoulder. Despite the bloat in my arms, I could probably reach around and grab it. Mr. Laurent is running in my direction, and by the time he's under me, I'm as high as a three-story house and moments away from puking.

"Use the gun!" he shouts again, pointing a finger at his head.

I know he wants me to harpoon myself so I'll fall to Earth along with that fat life insurance check, but I deliberately misinterpret him. He pointed the finger gun at his own head, after all. I should do as the boss says. My bloated arms feel tight as overripe melons, but I manage to pull the gun into place. Swallowing my nausea, I point the gun down at Mr. Laurent. Perhaps he can't see what I'm doing because he stands still, cranes his neck, and shields his eyes from the sun. I have only one harpoon, and I'll probably have to drop the gun after I shoot Mr. Laurent, but it'll be worth it. I'll figure out what to do with myself afterward.

I pull the trigger. The harpoon plunges straight between Mr. Laurent's eyes. His body falls and tugs the gun out of my hands. Even from this height, I can see his blood pooling on the yellow rocks below. The crew runs out of the cafeteria, gathers around the corpse, and looks up at me. Wouldn't expect the harpooner to be the floater, but here I am—a tiny, human blip rising into the low gray clouds.

I can't help but laugh. Moments before floating into oblivion, I did the right thing, ended that asshole's life. For the first time in months, I'm happy.

But floaters aren't supposed to be happy. Those wispy clouds aren't getting any closer. In fact, they're getting farther away. My skin loosens and no longer feels like it'll split at any second as my spherical body gradually reverts to its original shape. I'm drifting back to Earth, back to reality, too joyful for the clouds.

Below, the sirens are already screaming. Three cop cars and an ambulance speed down the dusty road, then screech into the employee parking lot. No one's ever seen a floater make it back down alive, but I'll be the first to do it. When my feet touch the ground, they'll be waiting for me with handcuffs, tasers, and pistols—the works. Life was miserable enough before I floated away, and it's about to get worse if I don't do something. Yet what is there to do? There are six cops and only one of me. I won't let them take me alive.

The pocket knife. I unhook it from my belt and, in my hurry, nearly drop it. It bounces from one clumsy inflated hand to the other before I grab it securely. I take a deep breath and look down. There's still a skyscraper of space between me and the ground. If I wait, my feet will touch down in ten minutes. But that's not the plan. I unfold the knife and point it at my swollen belly. Bile rises in my throat, and I puke all over my shirt. Soiled clothes won't matter anyway. I press the tip of the knife to my navel, shivering at the cold metal, then plunge it in. The air inside me blows out in a violent burst, spewing blood into the wind. The stab wound brings agony, but the deflation brings relief. As I deflate, my descent quickens. I'm no longer a helium balloon. I'm a meteor hurtling toward Earth.

I laugh in the face of death.

Boning

Sarcoma. Pretty name for a cancerous thing. Livia feels it suckling at her femur like an unwanted infant. She gets a sick joy from picking scabs and prodding bruises, but touching the tumor is excruciating. Agony pulses outward in tsunami-sized waves.

Eve sits beside Livia on the throw rug. She sniffles, then pulls her wife's hand away from the growth. Swelling is the only sign it's there under the skin and muscle. That and the doctor's report.

"Stop," Eve says. "It'll only make it worse."

"This sucks," Livia says. Her eyes are red and wet.

Eve wraps a blanket around both of them. Their pale breath becomes ice on the window pane. The house won't have heat until they scrounge up enough to pay the gas company, but the hospital bills take priority. Paying off the CT scans already cost them a vacation to New Orleans that had been three years in the making.

"I should call the Bone Man," Livia says.

Eve pulls out of their fleece cocoon. "That's a terrible idea."

"It's an affordable idea. You got a better one?"

Eve is silent. That's all the answer Livia needs.

***

They hear the Bone Man before he knocks. The clatter of his bones sounds like a stampede. Livia hobbles toward the door, but Eve beats her to it. In the doorway, she stands in front of her sick wife like a royal guard. The Bone Man rolls up the walkway, summoned by his symbol charcoaled beneath the welcome mat. He's big as a bull, but his shape oscillates between something humanoid and something chimeric. Whatever holds his skeleton together is a mystery. There's no skin to contain it, no ligaments to string one bone to the next. The bones aren't all human either. Eve could never hope to identify them, especially with their constant shaking. The Bone Man reaches the door, deflates like a pufferfish, and stops in place. His bones settle.

Livia squeezes into the doorway. Eve makes room but folds her arms together and glares at the visitor as if to say *Don't fuck with my girl.*

"Hello," Livia says, unsure if the Bone Man can respond.

The Bone Man says nothing. His skeleton rises and falls as if he were breathing, though he has no lungs.

"I …" Livia collects herself. "The doctor found cancer in my right femur. I need a new one."

Eve clears her throat. A signal.

"Oh right," Livia says. "*Please.*"

The magic word. It's the only cost for the Bone Man's services.

The Bone Man spins, slow as a lazy ceiling fan but soon building to a tornadic speed. A single bone extends from the whirlwind to touch Livia's leg. Feeling a tug, she winces, inches back, and considers making a full retreat. But the Bone Man's miracle is about to happen. She knows it. The whirlwind sucks out her festering femur. Eve squeezes Livia's shoulders to keep her upright. Livia's boneless thigh flops in the Bone Man's gale, but the flopping doesn't last long. A new bone dislodges from the whirlwind and bullets toward Livia. All she sees is a blur before it rebones her thigh. There's no blood. Not even a split in her jeans. Somehow the bone has found its place.

Livia can't look away from her leg. When she finally does, the Bone Man is gone, clattering off to his next appointment. Livia places her right foot on the ground to test the new femur. She bounces from foot to foot like a runner keeping her blood flowing at a stoplight. The fit feels funny, but what does it matter? She's cancer free. And before she can say anything, Eve grabs that bottle of wine they've been saving.

***

When Livia tells Dr. Simnitt about the Bone Man, his lips purse as if she'd mentioned seeing an energy healer.

"What did you expect?" he says. "Your new femur is a full inch shorter than your old one, which explains the limping and the pain. And if this X-ray says what I think it says, the Bone Man didn't actually fix your problem."

The vinyl examination table squeaks when Livia scoots forward. Her heart pumps into overdrive.

"What do you mean?" she asks.

"It looks like the sarcoma has spread to your tibia. We'll need a biopsy to be sure, but I'm almost certain that's what it is." Dr. Simnitt checks his watch, then stuffs the X-ray under his arm. "Instead of seeing the Bone Man again, how about you schedule a follow-up appointment? We have flexible payment plans, you know."

Livia sees only a wet blur as she pushes past the doctor and storms out the door. She has another call to make.

***

Eve isn't home from work yet. If everyone sticks to their schedule, she'll still be bartending a wedding reception when the Bone Man shows up at the house. Livia hopes he isn't late. It'd be awkward for Eve to step off the bus and see her wife getting another bone replacement. Livia didn't bother consulting her about it. After all, when she admitted that the femur fit poorly, Eve kicked a hole in the drywall and promised the next would be for the Bone Man's ivory balls. Unable to stand for long, Livia sits in a plastic chair on the porch. The windchill bites her exposed face and neck, but inside the house isn't much warmer. She doesn't have to wait long.

The Bone Man arrives right on time. He settles in front of her. A snow drift blows through his hollowness, but his bones remain still as if the cold means nothing to him.

"I know this is a lot to ask," Livia says from her seat. Putting even the smallest amount of weight on her leg feels like nerve electrocution. "But could you replace my right femur again? The one you gave me, it—"

The Bone Man has no head to shake, but he approximates the feeling of a shaking head. *No returns.*

Livia bites her lip and doesn't bother arguing. The Bone Man's rules are as ancient and unchanging as Holy Scripture. Still, it pains her to see half a dozen femurs floating inside his currently spherical form. They come in a variety of sizes, and from the looks of it, one would fit her perfectly. It's a carrot on a stick, and she's a limping donkey.

"Well, can you give me a new right tibia?" Livia asks. Near the Bone Man's not-head, several tibias lace together in a latticework pattern. "The doctor thinks my cancer has spread."

The Bone Man remains motionless. Then Livia remembers the magic word.

"Please."

The Bone Man starts spinning.

***

The femur is an inch too short, but that's no biggie compared to the tibia, which might have come from a horse. The bone crushes Livia's kneecap from below and her foot from above. The skin around it is bulbous and stretched. It reminds Livia of a video she once saw of a man putting rubber bands around a watermelon, one at a time, until it exploded. Her leg might well shower the living room with pink gore at any moment.

"Why the hell did you call him again?" Eve is crying.

"Give me more ice," Livia says. Two bags of peas rest on the coffee table, melted but close to freezing again in the house's chill.

Eve stomps to the freezer and finds a long-expired bag of frozen dinner rolls. She tosses them at Livia. Livia's leg twists as she shifts to catch the bag. She howls in anguish. Eve claps a hand over her mouth and rushes to her wife.

"Jesus Christ, I'm so sorry," she says. "I just—are you okay?"

"Of course I'm not fucking okay!"

Eve rubs Livia's back and leads her in deep breaths. The peak of Livia's agony passes.

"I can't go to work tomorrow," Livia says. "How am I supposed to lift boxes and—"

Eve shushes her. "We'll figure something out."

Silence fills the room, broken only by the groan of window panes straining against winter wind. The cold should numb Livia's pain, but it only makes her shiver, jostling oversized bone against raw nerve endings. She winces.

"Listen," she says. "I'm not an idiot. I checked to make sure the Bone Man had my size. But he gave me the wrong one anyway."

Eve says nothing, but she squeezes Livia's arm a little too hard.

Livia grimaces. "If you have something to say, stop crushing me and spit it out."

Eve's eyes burn with a fire hot enough to melt the ice on their windows.

"Let's call him up one more time," she says. "And if he doesn't fix this mess, I'll fucking kill him."

Livia smiles at her wife. For a moment, she's more awash in love than pain.

***

Eve schedules an appointment with the Bone Man. She buys the necessary intimidation materials the night before. Her credit card is maxed out, so she pawns her punk record collection and then heads to the hardware store. She's up late making the flame thrower and tending to Livia. Her wife's leg looks infected, skin gray-green and stretched so thin that her veins bulge outward, uncomfortably visible. Eve crushes up some painkillers, mixes them into a cup of chamomile, and gives Livia what little comfort she can. Livia takes small sips, but mostly she sweats and thrashes and screams at ghosts. Her condition deteriorates rapidly. There's no way they can afford a visit to the ER, but Eve knows they'll have to go even if the Bone Man fixes Livia. She sleeps fitfully for a couple hours, then wakes up early as a soldier preparing for battle.

Cold sunlight spills through the bedroom window and illuminates Livia's death-pale face. She blinks slowly through crusted eyes. Her chapped lips tremble. Eve sits beside her in bed.

"You trust me, right?" she asks, stroking her wife's hair. It's sweat-matted but glitters with ice crystals. This frigid house is no place for a sick woman.

Livia's voice comes out a low croak: "He's trying to turn me into a horse. I used to be one in a past life, but I don't want to be one anymore."

All Eve can do is nod. Livia's been spouting nonsense like this ever since her fever boiled over. A multi-day, bankrupting hospital stay is inevitable. Eve's intimidation tactics will have to go zero to sixty in three seconds.

There's no time for a slow-boil escalation in Livia's current state.

Eve waits on the front porch, gripping her homemade flamethrower. The internet taught her how to make this thing, but it didn't tell her how big the flame would be. She hopes it's big enough to engulf the Bone Man but not big enough to engulf the house. Her body shakes, partly from cold but mostly from nerves.

It's not long before the bony bastard rolls down the sidewalk toward the house. Eve almost pulls the trigger prematurely, but she breathes deep and forces herself to wait. She clears her throat and prepares a voice she's heard villains use in action movies. The Bone

Man rolls to a stop five feet away from her, waiting. Snow flurries drift to the ground around him.

"Hey, motherfucker." Eve hoists the flamethrower higher, struggling under its weight. "Either you give my wife a femur and tibia that actually fit, or I send your ass straight to Hell. What'll it be?"

The Bone Man is motionless.

Eve cocks her head and pops the bones in her neck with a satisfying crunch. The exercise of violent intimidation would be a lot more fun if the stakes weren't so high. She waits another ten seconds before asking again.

"Will you give her the bones or not?"

The Bone Man approximates a shaking head.

Eve's mouth hangs open as she fumbles for what to say. Ah, the magic word.

"Please?"

Another shake.

Tears trickle down Eve's cold, brown cheeks. She knows the Bone Man won't budge. Never in a million years. And Livia will either get her leg amputated or die of infection. Eve can picture a life of financial ruin plenty well, but a life without Livia is harder to imagine. Nine years together since they first met at Pride. Seven since they got married in an aviary. Five since they decided kids were out of the question; the lovers would live only for each other.

Eve sniffles, then raises the flamethrower: "So be it."

The fiery explosion propels her backward through the window. She falls on her ass in the living room. Her ears ring. With double vision, she surveys the damage. There's broken glass everywhere and cuts on her arm, but everything else looks fine.

Through the bedroom door, she sees Livia resting as if she hadn't even heard the explosion. The sight sends a jolt of fear through Eve until she sees the rise and fall of Livia's chest. Her wife is comatose but alive. Eve hopes the same can't be said for the Bone Man. She stands up, staggers toward the door, and opens it to the outside.

Neighbors in bathrobes are on their porches with hands over their mouths and phones pressed to their ears. The police will be here soon. Through a curtain of falling snow, Eve scans her burning yard for the Bone Man. She spies a flaming rib by the sundered oak tree and a smoking skull by what once was the mailbox. She pumps her fist in victory. That skeletal fucker, wasted.

Except not. His undestroyed bits—shrunk to the size of a poodle—emerge from behind a truck with its alarm blaring. Eve freezes. She has no plan B. What's left of the Bone Man rolls toward her like a ghoulish soccer ball. Eve backs up, but not quick enough. The Bone Man starts spinning before she can take shelter. He churns faster and faster. When he touches her, she feels his supernatural pull—the pain of 206 simultaneous tuggings. The Bone Man plucks her skeleton apart, piece by piece. She feels a pinch in her spinal cord as her vertebrae joins his cyclonic form, a softening in her hand as her finger bones vanish, and a deflation in her head as her skull becomes his. She transforms into something sluglike, folds of clothing and skin covering scarcely protected organs, more puddle than human. She'd scream if she could, but the neighbors do it for her. Blaring sirens cut through the icy pink morning. Inside the house, Livia mutters feverish delusions about past lives, oblivious to the state of her wife.

And when the Bone Man integrates all of Eve's skeleton, he rises up, grown to the size of a great Dane. Then, off he goes, clattering down the scorched sidewalk toward the next desperate soul.

HEIRLOOMS

(First published in *Fingers*)

I found Grandma Florence's pinky finger in the garbage bin, shriveled and dry like a worm fried on a summer sidewalk. I must have stared at it for a while because Liam, my partner on the garbage collection route, asked what the holdup was. We still had four hundred properties to get through.

"Gimme a minute," I said. The squeak of Grandma's porch swing caught my attention. She'd been watching me at work. "Grandma, is this—"

"I can't hear you, dear," she said. "Come closer."

She beckoned me with a four-fingered hand. Shuddering, I imagined jumping on the truck, slapping its metal side, and screaming, "Go, go go!" But this was Grandma, harmless as ever. I jogged up to her house.

A walker sat next to the porch swing. Grandma wore a long black dress, and her perfume smelled like honeysuckle. The contrast struck me as odd. I glanced at where her pinky used to be. The nub was smooth and pale. It was as if Grandma had popped her pinky off like a doll's limb, exposing shiny plastic beneath.

"What happened?" I asked, trying to keep cool.

"All my life, I held my pinky up ladylike," she said. "Your grandfather expected that of me, but what does his opinion matter now? I'm done being dainty."

"Grandma, are you …"

Liam honked the truck's booming horn. I held up a finger as if to say *one minute* but dropped it quickly. Using my fingers felt weird all of a sudden.

"You should visit more," Grandma said. "You only come by for my trash."

It was true. Ever since Grandpa died, I'd found it hard to be in the same room with Grandma. Every conversation revolved around her regrets. *If divorce had been acceptable back then … If I'd only gone to Italy … If I hadn't had your father so young …* It had gotten to the point where I ducked her phone calls and ignored her voicemails. Listening to them only ever made me feel sad and guilty.

"I have to go, Grandma," I said. There was no good way to extricate myself from the conversation.

She nodded, and it was either her neck that creaked or the chipped porch swing. I returned to my post and took one more look at the pinky before dumping it. As the truck pulled away with me hanging off the side, I glanced back at Grandma. Blank-faced, she waved with her mutilated hand.

***

The next week, two more fingers appeared in the trash: ring and index. I hadn't told anyone about the pinky. My mom had enough to worry about with chemo, and Liam, well, he would've just taken a picture and posted it to his "Another Man's Trash" blog among pics of scrapped antique furniture and battleworn dildos. I'd deal with this crisis myself.

"Grandma," I said, cupping her detached fingers in my gloved hand. "Why did—"

Liam honked before I could finish the thought. I yelled at him to wait. When I looked back at Grandma, she was smiling with her eyes closed, absorbing the golden sunrise and chickadee songs.

"You shouldn't be hurting yourself like this," I said.

"It doesn't hurt, dear." She wriggled her doll-smooth nubs. Only her middle finger and thumb remained, her hand mangled into a perpetually rude gesture. "The marriage finger and the finger your Grandfather used to point at me when I'd done something wrong. Or what he considered wrong, anyway: putting my feet on the coffee table, talking at dinner, going out with the girlfriends." She admired her hand. "It's a beautiful absence."

"It's wrong, Grandma. It's … it's fucked up."

I'd never cursed in front of her before, but I wanted to emphasize my seriousness, to meet her transgression with my own. Grandma only laughed, her eye wrinkles deepening into shadowed canyons.

"Wish I could've been the type to go around swearing," she said. "Smoking and drinking and dancing and fucking. What a life he robbed me of. It's too late now."

My cheeks flushed. Unsure how to respond, I walked back to the truck. I'd call Mom this time. If she was having one of her good days, she'd be able to help.

***

Grandma's thumb and middle finger were next, but this time she placed them on top of the garbage bin instead of inside it. When I arrived for trash pick up, she was standing beside the bin, shooing away hungry crows. The truck hissed to a stop, and I jumped off it.

Only then did I notice that the fingers were tied together with a glossy green ribbon.

"Seriously, Grandma, you can't keep doing this," I said. "Mom knows about it. Or at least I think she does. I left a voicemail."

"These ones are gifts for you," Grandma said. "Heirlooms."

My job might've given me a strong stomach, but her words cut straight through my two years of experience working in the grotesque. I lowered my voice so Liam wouldn't hear me.

"You need help," I said. "We can find a home that will—"

"There's no need for that. I won't be around long enough," she said, speaking just as loud as before. She scooped the heirlooms into her fingerless hand, and I couldn't understand why she didn't do it with her intact one. "Consider these symbols of how I would've liked to live. The middle finger is self-explanatory. The thumb is a hitchhiker's thumb. Or it would've been if things had been different."

"Grandma," I said. Tears boiled in my eyes.

"Enjoy your life, Kai," she said. "And don't look inside the bin next Monday."

***

I didn't look inside the bin. All I knew was that it was heavier than usual and smelled like honeysuckle. Grandma wasn't sitting on the porch. Maybe I should've called Mom again, but she hadn't gotten out of bed in a week and it was too late to do anything anyway.

"Bin's empty," I told Liam through the ball in my throat.

"Alright, let's keep going," he replied.

I hopped onto the truck and sobbed, hoping Liam wouldn't hear me over the rumbling engine. The two fingers in my pocket were my only comfort. I squeezed them. The only thing she and I shared was regret.

'Til the Sun Wheel Turns No More

(First published in *ANTIFA SPLATTERPUNK*)

When the first band loaded their equipment onto the stage, I gaped at the sun wheel decorating their bass drum. Some might think it was a cool design and nothing more, but anyone with an interest in history and a desire not to repeat it would shudder at the sight.

"Why'd you tell Bo we'd play this show?" I asked Milo.

Milo sucked the froth from his beer, wiped his mustache, and shrugged. "How was I supposed to know?"

Before I could ask if he'd done any research on the bands—any at all, goddamnit—some bald giant slapped Milo on the back. Milo turned, grinned at the guy, and gave a quick *skål* as they clinked glasses.

"Hans, what the fuck's up, man?" Milo asked.

This was the first I'd ever heard of Hans. I turned toward the metal band stickers plastered in thick, peeling layers on the wall.

"Let me buy you a drink, Milo," Hans said. He didn't bother to ask my name or look at me. "We'll catch up while Hemlandskrig plays. You're on second, right?"

Jesus, I thought. *With a name like 'homeland's war,' how could Milo NOT realize they were Nazis?*

Milo nodded at Hans and held up his index finger while he pounded the rest of his drink. Then off they went to the bar, leaving me alone among the Nazis. I'd stay there just long enough to get my cut—enough to cover overdue rent, I hoped—and then bounce. I shuffled to the corner, away from everyone else, and took a seat on a torn vinyl stool with exposed yellow stuffing. No beer to keep my hands preoccupied—I never drank before shows— I drummed the beat of our new song on my thighs. Milo and Hans chatted it up at the bar. I couldn't hear what they were saying, but their expressive gestures and wide smiles suggested they'd been friends for ages.

I'd known Milo since secondary school a decade back. Our boyhood bond was primarily musical, but it ran deeper than that. In high school, a bully took particular interest in me and would beat my ass any chance he got. Milo wasn't physically strong enough to defend me, but he had his dad's collection of occult spell books to aid in our revenge. He invited me over one afternoon to put a curse on my bully. I thought it was silly and pointless, but the next day, my bully didn't show up to school. He'd broken both of his arms in a bike accident. Never again would his fists bruise me, and never again would I underestimate the occult.

Given our deep friendship, it bothered me that Milo had never once mentioned Hans to me. Hans who—based on how he made Milo snort-laugh beer out of his nose—probably played a bigger role in Milo's life than I did. A pang of jealousy coursed through me, something more than platonic—a desire for Milo a decade in the making. I shoved it down and tuned out my surroundings.

Hemlandskrig played ten minutes later. Their scrawny vocalist Henrik Strid, wearing his own band's shirt, growled out the title of their first song: "FOURTEEN EIGHTY EIIIIIIIIIGHT." Nazis loved that number like stoners loved 420. And if the sun wheel and the band name had been the first two strikes against them, this title was the definitive third. I stood up to leave, then stopped when the first riff kicked in. The guitar was catchy, aggressive, and deliciously evil. Blistering blast beats added a layer of brutal intensity, and the vocals were nothing short of a dissonant, alluring incantation. A weak part of me wanted to stay—*just for the music, not the politics*, as my teenage self would've said. How many shows like this had I gone to in high school just so to enjoy a night of headbanging away from my homophobic dad's house? I didn't have that excuse anymore.

I pushed through the jam of sweaty, foul-smelling fascists on my way to the door. Pressing skin-to-skin with them made me squirm. Milo was still talking to Hans at the bar, a hand cupped over his mouth so they could hear each other over the music. Hans listened closely while bobbing his head to the song. The sight made me bristle. I tried to slip away without either of them noticing, but Milo tapped my shoulder.

"Hey," he said. "You going out for a smoke?"

"No, I'm going home."

"What? Why?" Milo's face contorted. His cheeks flushed red with booze.

"Why the fuck do you think, man?"

Milo shook his head. His eyes were flat as he spoke to me in monotone: "Really could've used the money, but fine, I'll tell Bo. Later, Jonas."

I slipped into the brisk October night, feeling like a dog with his tail between his legs.

***

I drank alone in my studio apartment after the show, and as often happens when drinking alone, I did something stupid. Most of the time that meant buying dumb shit online—a sound system I couldn't afford or a rare collector's edition of a Bruce Lee movie I already owned—but this was a whole new level of idiocy. Half a handle of whiskey deep, I pulled out the occult spell book Milo had loaned me. It was a crumbling tome bound in toad leather and filled with the kind of spells you wouldn't catch Gandalf casting. Even Milo, who wasn't above cursing people, told me not to use it. The tome was to remain a museum piece and nothing more.

Sprawled out on the carpet, I flipped through the yellowed pages, struggling to read the hand-inked text through my bleary vision. The night's events also compromised my focus. I fumed thinking about Hemlandskrig's massive Nazi fanbase ... and boiled with shame remembering how much I'd loved their music. I wondered if Milo and Hans were still enjoying themselves at the bar. Maybe they'd even joined the crowd for some headbanging, though I hoped Milo had the conscience to stay away. Maybe the booker—one band short—had given Hemlandskrig the go-ahead to play an extended set. An extra twenty minutes of hate from their back catalogue.

These hypotheticals fueled my rage—and my drinking. The booze stopped burning my throat. My brain stopped recording memories. Whatever happened after that first bottle was banished to some lightless corner of my mind. But the specifics of my actions didn't matter. What mattered were the deadly consequences.

***

The next morning, while gripping the toilet seat and barfing liquid fire, I noticed my new injuries. Blood leaked from the pads of three fingers on my left hand, all three drops falling in synchrony. If it weren't for my frying-pan-to-the-fucking-skull migraine and the fact that I had no idea why I was bleeding, the drip might have hypnotized me. I lifted myself to the sink, then shuddered as a new wave of nausea hit me. Eyes closed, I took a deep breath in hopes that it'd settle my stomach. It didn't, so I tried to ignore the discomfort while I washed my wounds. My blood swirled down the drain. In its absence, there were three X-shaped cuts on each finger. Any time I pulled them out of the running water, the blood welled up again. Looking at it made my head feel light. I bandaged the wounds, then stumbled to my living room to find an explanation. It didn't take long.

The spell book. A broken whiskey bottle, glass jagged and red. Countless bloody fingerprints crusting the gray carpet black. That part confused me. If the blood had already dried, did that mean I'd been bleeding all night? I wasn't hemophilic. My blood should have clotted by now. I examined the bandages. Miniscule beads of blood already penetrated the surface. I sighed and my breath tasted like acid.

That's when my pinky started burning. Literally. The tan bandage blackened, warped, and smoked with the glow of the bloody X beneath. I grunted and squeezed my pinky, but the pain brought me to my knees. A minute of writhing and a mouthful of frothy puke later, the burning subsided. I took a long breath before removing the bandage. It came off like super glue, peeling skin away with it. I winced before going wide eyed. The X had cauterized, leaving pink, white, and gray skin pink beneath. The raised scar reminded me of the bumps on a topographical globe. My pinky pad was numb to all sensation, but blood still dripped from two other fingers on my left hand.

"What the fuck?" I said.

My phone vibrated and I jumped. Without even checking, I knew it was work. The record shop needed an employee for its oh-so-busy Tuesday morning.

I triple-wrapped my fingers—even the cauterized one—before dashing out the door, determined to save my job and forget the past twenty-four hours.

***

Karin smirked as I entered the record shop, the bell above the door announcing my lateness.

"Hey," she said. "If I can stay up until 3 a.m. and still make it to work on time the next day, then so can you."

"I wasn't up that late," I said. "Turned in early, actually."

"Huh." Karin squinted, then shook her head. "Must have been the beer goggles. Could've sworn I saw you. Anyway, you hear the good news?"

She propped her feet up on the cash register.

"No, what?" I walked behind the register and punched my time card, leaving a bloody fingerprint behind.

"Henrik Strid is dead."

It took me a second to place the name. *Henrik Strid.* The vocalist of Hemlandskrig. I stood there, blinking rapidly and unable to speak. Karin took the time card from me and put it back in the metal rack. When I remained silent, she waved a hand in front of my face.

"Not even a smile, Jonas?" she said. "Asshole got what was coming to him."

"How'd he die?"

"Normally I wouldn't get excited about this sort of thing, but …" Karin typed something on her phone, then held the cracked screen in front of my face.

I jerked backward. Whoever captured the gruesome shot had done so from behind police tape. A limbless corpse rested at the center of Stallgatan, the street slick with red pulp. The body had exactly two identifiable features: a Hemlandskrig t-shirt and an X-shaped patch of flesh missing from the forehead. My gut twisted. I lifted a hand to my mouth and turned away.

"Jesus," Karin shook her head and put her phone away. "You'll look at the suicide photo on Mayhem's *Dawn of the Black Hearts* like it's nothing, but the second I show you a mutilated Nazi, you get squeamish. What's the—"

"Listen," I said. "I was late because I was puking this morning. Can I go home? The shop's not even busy right now."

Karin squinted for a long moment, then punched my time card for me. She looked down at it.

"A whole three minutes on the clock. Should buy you half a candy bar."

"Yup." I was already headed out the door. "See you tomorrow."

I walked to the subway, shaking the whole way there, blood dripping from my useless bandages.

***

I texted Milo about Henrik but didn't get a response. By the time we next talked, a second person had been murdered: Anders Viklund. He was the vocalist of the notorious Nazi black metal band Chamber of Annihilation. He'd also done time for stalking his ex-girlfriend. It was in prison that he'd recorded his one-man "magnum opus," which was really just some poorly mixed, unlistenable racist dogshit. He'd only been a free man for two months when police found his body atop a light post, impaled through the asshole. Electricity from the shattered fixture had fried his skin black and burned his clothes off. A carved "X" decorated his exposed skull. The coroner was only able to identify him from his wallet, which had fallen to the sidewalk below. Anders's murder, like Henrik's, had taken place on a heavily trafficked street, and also like Henrik's, produced no witnesses. Not only that, the street cameras had malfunctioned, leaving the police with no leads. They'd noticed the "X" left on each victim but hadn't yet made the Nazi connection.

When I checked my phone, social media was flooded with news, panic, and speculation. It had been ages since the last highly publicized black metal murder, and this strange, gruesome case captured everyone's attention.

I was the only one with the truth. When my bleeding thumb wound cauterized itself and woke me from a fitful sleep, I knew what had happened. Not the who, where, and how, but those details would come soon. It was an hour later, after I'd called in sick and poured myself a hair of the dog, that police announced Anders's death. I sat on my couch, eyes glazed over, watching the live footage on TV. The reporters didn't show the body, but the pictures had already leaked, blowing up true crime forums with speculation about a new serial killer. When I saw the pictures, more images flashed through my mind: a long-haired man stumbling past parked cars, a street lamp glowing piss-yellow, and a violent shower of sparks. The flashes existed somewhere between my own memory and someone—or some*thing*—else's. I shuddered.

I should've felt happy. Fascist assholes were dropping like flies. They'd never vandalize another synagogue or beat the shit out of another immigrant minding their own business. But for all the times I'd extolled the virtues of killing Nazis, I'd never seen myself summoning a demon to hunt them down. Did that make me a hypocrite? A coward? The thought tormented me.

I needed a distraction. Loud, angry music. I texted Milo about an impromptu band practice.

I made a sandwich, threw on a jacket, then walked to the rehearsal space we shared with three other bands. The entrance was accessible only through a tight alleyway with a laundromat on one side and a vintage clothing boutique on the other. Our band had received countless noise complaints from those businesses over the years, and I figured we'd receive another for practicing in the middle of the day. The boutique owner, smoking and leaning against the brick wall, scowled when I approached the door. I nodded an apology at her, then reached into my jacket for the key.

Except my fingers didn't grip cool metal. Whatever they found was warm, spongy, and sticky. I held it for a long moment, wondering if meat from my sandwich had fallen into my pocket, but something told me that wasn't the case. I turned away from the boutique owner before pulling out the mystery object.

Unclenching my fist, I discovered not one, but two fleshy X's. Each had porcelain pale skin with a bloody red underside. Yellow clumps of fat still clung to the scraps. The X's squelched as they settled in my hand. The sound made me gag. I clasped a hand over my mouth and closed my eyes, scarcely able to process the horrible discovery. I shoved the X's back in my pocket and fumbled for the key beneath them. Hopefully the boutique owner hadn't witnessed anything.

Hand shaking, it took several tries to unlock the door. As soon as it opened, I rushed inside and collapsed beside my drum set. I wheezed, trying and failing to stave off a panic attack. What if Milo came in and saw me like this? Would he consider my drunken revenge against the Nazis as justified as my bully revenge ten years back? I wracked my brain for any memory of the last two nights. I couldn't remember killing Henrik and Anders, but here I was with scraps of their flesh, trophies from the hunt. Had the demon possessed my body in order to kill these men? Or had I killed them of my own volition and suppressed the memory? Maybe Karin *had* seen me that night, shuffling toward my victim in a fugue state, magical or otherwise. I didn't have time to consider the possibilities. Milo would be here any minute.

On cue, he staggered into the rehearsal space just as I reached the sink, my fingers sticky with both my blood and the blood of two dead men. Milo gripped the door frame and watched me. Even from ten feet away, he stank of rum.

"What are you doing?" he asked. His voice was flat, lobotomized. He only sounded that way when he was off his antidepressants.

Though I'd successfully hidden a decade of feelings for Milo, I was a bad liar in all other respects. The longer I held back the truth, the bigger the ball in my throat grew, choking me from the inside. I couldn't keep it inside any longer. Not in front of my best friend.

"I killed them," I said. "Or, at least, they're dead because of me."

Milo's eyes went glassy. He blinked hard to clear them. And though he probably knew the answer, he asked the question anyway: "Who?"

"Henrik and Anders. I … they deserved it, right?" My voice cracked like I was fifteen again. "I mean, they're fucking Nazis. The book you lent me, it … it did the job."

Milo let out a sob, then grunted and wiped his cheek as if to correct himself. He paced a moment before ripping a Krallice poster off the wall and kicking over my snare.

"What the hell, man?" I said, holding out my bloody hands to stop him.

"Don't fucking touch me!" he said, angrier than he'd ever sounded when screaming our band's songs. "You … you didn't know them like I did."

I froze, unable to process his words. Surely I'd misheard him.

On the wall behind him, where the poster had been, a dark shape materialized, a thousand drops of oil seeping through the drywall and coalescing into a single shape. A slick shadow lurking over Milo's shoulder. Before I could warn him, he stormed out of the room and slammed the door behind him. The shadow receded back into the wall, midnight black diluting to dishwater gray and finally to a scuffed white. Whatever it was had vanished, at least for now. I stood there, trembling, trying to erase the last minute from my memory. But deep down I knew my eyes and ears could be trusted. Milo, the betrayer, hexed, stalked, and soon-to-be-doomed.

It was my turn to cry.

***

Since I—or the demon possessing me—only killed when I slept, I decided not to sleep. Amphetamines from the dealer down the hall helped. I remember the look on his face when I bought out his stock. An expression that asked *Are you sure about that, man?* until I pulled out the fat wad of cash I'd earned from selling my most treasured black metal records earlier that day. I'd only ever bought weed from the guy, so this new purchase felt like skipping a half-dozen steps in the road to fucking up my life.

My first yawn of the evening was my signal to snort a line. The effects were immediate: heart galloping like a racehorse, energy surging through me, and self-confidence building exponentially. It was the kind of confidence Milo exuded when speaking to anyone, Nazi friends included. But I couldn't let myself dwell on his betrayal.

The next several hours were a blur. I tossed the X-shaped skin scraps in my garbage disposal, ground them into paste, and washed them down the drain. I let the faucet run extra long to make sure it got everything. But even with the most damning evidence gone, I couldn't be sure what still lingered in my apartment. I scrubbed and vacuumed the carpet, laser-focused on cleansing every square inch. Any stain that looked like blood—though perhaps it was actually pizza sauce or wine—I scoured out of existence. Whenever my still-bleeding middle finger re-stained the carpet, I cursed and cleaned with even more intensity. The next time I looked at a clock, it was midnight. I snorted a second line before going out on the balcony to burn any clothes that might've come in contact with blood.

My mind returned to Milo as the band patches sewn to my jacket curled and blackened in the grill's flame. We'd gone to countless shows over the past ten years, headbanging too close to the monitors, getting drunk off our asses, and then stumbling home to watch '80s B-movies until we passed out around sunrise. Had Milo's fascist mask never slipped in all the time we'd spent together? Maybe my feelings for him had blinded me to the rot behind his charming smile.

A knock on the door jolted me into the present. I'd been lost in thought for God knows how long, and my patch jacket had disintegrated into ash. Faint embers still burned near the bottom of the grill, so I slammed the metal lid shut to cover any remaining evidence. Sneaking back inside my apartment, I kicked the rest of my drug stash under the couch before picking up a kitchen knife. A visitor at 1 a.m. was never a good thing. The bleach-smelling carpet quieted my approach. My breath fast and shallow, I looked through the door's peephole.

It was Milo, swaying side to side, looking even drunker than he'd been at our abortive band practice twelve hours earlier. He wore a Hemlandskrig shirt, tattered enough to be several years old. I bit my lip to keep from crying.

"What the fuck do you want?" I asked, hating the tremble in my voice.

"I'm here for murder tips," Milo shouted loud enough to wake my neighbors. Maybe that was his intention. "I hear you've got some great ones."

I clenched the knife's handle, then glanced through the peephole to check Milo for weapons. For a split second, that large, amorphous shadow appeared behind him, darker than a winter night. It disappeared when I blinked. Still, I couldn't excuse it as an eyelash obscuring my vision or a light in the hallway shorting out and coming back on. I knew exactly what it was. A shiver coursed through me.

"Aren't you going to invite me in? I'm ready to be murdered, too." Milo's head lolled as he slurred his words. Another minute of this and there'd be neighbors poking their heads into the hall and police cars lighting up my window.

I whipped open the door and pulled Milo inside. He tripped and fell face-first onto the floor. Grunting, he pulled himself up, saliva stringing his slack mouth to the carpet. I hid my knife in the back of my waistband.

"So, what, are you here to avenge your Nazi friends?" I swallowed hard. "You're drunk, man. You can't do shit."

I don't know why I provoked him or what my endgame was. All I knew was that I wanted everything to be over: the spell, the murders, our friendship like a house built on swampland and rapidly sinking. I wanted a life outside of deception, guilt, and—luck willing—prison.

Before Milo could reply, the shadow squeezed under the door, undeniably real this time. It stretched into my living room slow as a lava flow and just as dangerous.

Milo must have seen my wide-eyed panic because he turned around. He gave no reaction, just looked back at me as if I were out of my mind.

Inch by inch, the shadow wriggled across the floor, curled up at its pulsing edges. I almost said something when it slithered between Milo's legs, but I knew it wouldn't do any good. Milo was blind to the shadow, and the shadow didn't pay him any mind. I was its target. It approached me, twitching and sluglike.

"You're going away for a long time, motherfucker," Milo said. "Before you killed him, Anders told me all about prison. Plenty of guys like him there who'd love to slit your—"

The shadow gripped my feet. It sizzled like broiling meat as it climbed my leg. The sensation ripped a memory from the recesses of my mind, and I knew then that I'd felt this twice before. I smacked the attacker through my jeans, but what felt like sharp suckers hooked into my thigh. I pulled the knife from my waistband and cut through the denim, sawing at the muscular shadow below. Milo squinted and backed away. I didn't speak, but my eyes begged him for help. He took another step toward the door. At my next attack, the shadow burst with volcanic heat. I screamed as my thigh burned and the knife's metal melted into globs of dripping steel. Nothing I'd done had harmed the shadow. It was invincible.

"What the fuck ..." Milo pressed his back against the door, frozen.

The agony gave way to a dissociated fog as I watched myself struggle from the outside. It didn't matter that I was awake; the shadow would gain control over me just as it had the past two nights. And there was Milo, easy prey, too captivated and shitfaced to flee. He'd die here and maybe I'd even get away with it. After all, the shadow had ensured there were no witnesses and no cameras for the last two murders. Why would Milo's be any different? My soul floated farther from my body like an untethered astral projection. But harnessing all of my willpower, I merged with my body once more, feeling the crushing density of two beings occupying one vessel.

The shadow thrashed inside me, whipped my soul with its thousand razored tentacles. All I had was a moment to act. Even with Milo's betrayal, I couldn't stand to see him splattered across every wall in my apartment.

"Go!" I grunted. "I don't want to kill you."

Milo didn't budge. Couldn't. But there was still a way to save him. My pinky and thumb scars had both cauterized, but the "X" on my middle finger still bled. I raised it to my mouth in a jerky motion, the shadow resisting me every inch. Maybe it knew what I was about to do. Finger between my teeth, I closed my eyes and overrode the part of my brain that cared about self-preservation. The black tentacles wriggled upward, circling my torso, my chest, and my arm. This would be my only chance. I bit down hard. My front teeth cracked when they hit bone, but I muscled through the pain and kept clamping down, shaking my head like a wolf snapping a rabbit's neck. Jets of blood squirted into my nostrils and down my chin. Tendons squelched and popped. I howled through gritted, splintered teeth to cover the sound. Just as the tentacles reached my wrist, there was one final pop like a rubber band snapping. My middle finger fell to the floor. The shadow shriveled, loosened its grip, and shrunk to the size of a worm. Jerking deathlike toward my finger, it wrapped around the small sacrifice and burst into flames. It burned a blindingly bright green, then extinguished in an instant, leaving the finger's X-shaped wound as a cauterized scar.

The shadow was gone, but Milo was still there, huddled in a corner and gaping at me. I held his gaze for a moment before collapsing.

The next thing I remember was waking up in the hospital alone.

***

I ran into Milo again at a black metal show a year later. Seeing him across the bar sent a wave of panic through me, and I Googled the bands playing that night to make sure they weren't Nazis. No red flags popped up in my research, so I stayed, albeit far away from Milo. We stood on opposite sides of the room for the first band's set. It felt so different from when we used to crowd the stage and throw up horns for every song. Alone, we sipped our beers and pretended to ignore each other.

I contemplated leaving after the first band, but Milo approached me before I could sneak away. His shoulders were hunched. His eye contact faltered. I'd never seen him so awkward, and it gave me a strange sort of comfort.

"Hey," he said.

I chugged the last of my beer, preparing my exit. Just as I turned around, he grabbed my arm, but his touch was light, almost gentle. I waited for him to speak.

"I want you to know that I don't fuck with those guys anymore," he said. "The ones who are still alive, I mean. Don't fuck with their politics either."

I nodded for a long moment before saying anything. "Cool, man."

"Can I ..." He scratched his neck. "Can I buy you a drink?"

My cheeks flushed. Since the last time I saw him, Milo had grown a beard and styled his blonde hair into a back bun. He looked cute. But I couldn't get sucked in again. Not after everything.

"Listen," I said. "I'm proud of you, but, uh ... no. You understand how it is, right?"

He nodded a little too long, then cleared his throat.

"Yeah," he said. "I get it. Well, uh ... I'll be seeing you."

"Right," I replied. "Have a nice life."

"You, too."

That was the last time we spoke. On occasion, I think of Milo, our last conversation. I hope, for all our sakes, that people really can change.

The Last of Her Kind

(First published in *Field Notes from a Nightmare*)

The last rhinos had armed guards to protect them from poachers, but the last red-ringed owl had something better: birders. Dozens pointed their binoculars at the cottonwood tree the owl called home. These sworn protectors observed at all hours, rarely straying from their posts.

As such, Hudson Wallace took extra precautions when poisoning the bird, knowing damn well the consequences of getting caught. He slathered a toxic paste on the backs of mice he'd bought at the pet store. The mice couldn't reach the poison and chew it away, which was vital since the owl would only go for live prey.

A birder once saw Hudson releasing the mice and asked what he was doing.

"They're an endangered pygmy species," Hudson said. He'd rehearsed the lie enough that it rolled easy off the tongue. "The university is breeding them and reintroducing them into the wild."

Knowing jack shit about unfeathered animals, the birder smiled, nodded, and returned her attention to Alice. That was what she called the owl. Hudson thought it was a dumb name—too human. Like naming a dog 'John' or 'Mary.' But the name didn't matter. What mattered was that Alice joined Hudson's natural history museum as its next big attraction, one he planned to call "The Last of Her Kind."

The museum had been his family's pride and joy for ninety years. However, it wouldn't reach its centennial unless something changed. The adjacent highway had closed for repairs after last year's floods and showed no signs of reopening soon. Most of the museum's traffic had come from travelers who needed a bathroom break and something interesting to look at—a stop of convenience rather than intent. Only the truly bored would navigate rough back roads to see the museum's crumbling taxidermy displays and brochures full of outdated science facts.

Despite the museum's shoddiness, Hudson couldn't let it go. He'd spent so much of his childhood running tours with his mother, relishing the moments when their tag-team approach made tour groups go wide-eyed with fascination. "What should you do if a mountain lion attacks you?" his mother would ask, pointing to the taxidermied beast frozen in a ferocious pounce. She'd let the question linger a moment, then turn to her son. Hudson would smile, raise his arms above his head, and roar as loud as possible. It always made the crowd jump, then laugh.

At his mother's funeral six months back, Hudson had vowed to preserve the woman's legacy. That meant keeping the struggling museum open at all costs. His initial efforts were nothing unusual: buying online ads only to discover he'd lost more money than he'd made, applying for a historic landmark grant only to find the program had ironically been slashed to pay for flood damages, and finally, begging for an early inheritance from his great-aunt only to discover she'd used it to pay for hip surgery.

The Alice idea came next. An old high school friend posted an article about her on social media, and "The Last of Her Kind" vision popped into Hudson's head instantly. It was an intrusive thought that turned his gut but couldn't be banished. He spent weeks racking his brain for a better idea, but no alternative came. So it was that he bought his first box of mice and a barrel of sharp-smelling pest poison.

The mice releases went on for weeks. A few owls died, but none of them were Alice. Hudson knew to be patient. The mice he'd poisoned and released made up only a small percentage of those living in the woods. However, the longer this hunt went on, the higher his anxiety climbed. What if Alice took the bait but died when he wasn't around? What if someone else collected her corpse first? Consumed with worry, Hudson spent more and more time away from the museum, worsening the financial problems that had led him to desperate measures in the first place. He assured himself it would be worth it. Birders would pay big money to see Alice up close and personal, even after she'd passed.

Her death came at the perfect time. It was March and the sandhill cranes were migrating through Nebraska, momentarily pulling the birding community westward. During this moment of peace, Alice enjoyed her last supper. Hudson watched through night vision goggles as she devoured the mouse and, minutes later, spewed her guts in an attempted cleansing. But the poison had already seeped into her veins. Alice fell from her cottonwood perch and thumped to the ground, motionless. Hudson approached through a patch of nettles and scanned the area for birders. Seeing no binoculars glinting in the moonlight, he rushed toward Alice. He would've scooped her into his backpack right then, but her beauty caught him off guard. Red ringlets decorated her body from head to talon. The white plumage around her neck ruffled in the midnight breeze. Her still-open eyes glowed gold. A terrible heat welled up inside Hudson's throat, but he didn't have time to process the feeling. He bagged Alice, then ran to his car parked a half-mile off. No one chased him, but he sprinted as if his life depended on it, slowing only when he realized the jostling might damage his feathered treasure.

In the car, he took a minute to catch his breath, then drove away at five under the speed limit. He'd traveled through Nebraska with two ounces of Colorado weed before, but his nerves then paled to how he felt now with Alice in the passenger seat. That said, cops weren't conservationists. If they pulled him over and saw the owl, he'd claim it was roadkill he'd picked off the highway like a good citizen. Maybe they'd give him a weird look, but scraping dead animals off the blacktop was hardly a criminal offense. His heartbeat slowed.

He pulled into the museum's tiny parking lot twenty minutes later. 'Platte Museum of Natural History,' the faded sign read. As soon as Alice started making him money, he'd get a flashier sign. He'd pay the past-due property taxes, get the plumbing fixed, and change out those half-dozen flickering fluorescents. Maybe he'd even pay a scientist to fact-check his yellowing brochures.

"You've saved me, Alice," Hudson said, stroking the backpack.

The canvas twitched. Hudson froze. If Alice was still alive, he didn't know if he'd have the guts to kill her with his bare hands. He unzipped the backpack slowly, prepared to zip it back up at the first sign of thrashing wings. But the bird inside was motionless. He pressed a finger to her chest and felt no pulse. Just the stillness of extinction.

***

Normally, Hudson did taxidermy for the museum himself, but given how one-of-a-kind Alice was, he hired someone more experienced this time. The bill would be exorbitant, but he'd pay it off with all the money Alice would bring in. The finished product arrived a week later. Alice was positioned with her wings splayed and talons outstretched as if diving for the kill. She looked alive in this pose. Hudson shuddered.

Word spread quickly. Hundreds of birders flocked to the museum. Some even wore funeral clothes for the occasion. Hudson knew the visitors would come with questions about how Alice died and wound up in his possession, so, as with all his lies, he rehearsed this one until it felt true.

"We weren't sure how it happened until the taxidermist found the tumor. Poor Alice had cancer," Hudson explained.

The tour group listened with rapt attention. So many visitors were packed into the space that Hudson sweated from the heat of their collective bodies. One guest stood half in the bathroom to make room for everyone. Another squeezed shoulder-to-shoulder with a stuffed mountain lion that had seen better days.

"How'd she end up in your museum?" one of the visitors asked.

"I was the one who found her," Hudson said. A sensation like hot coals traveled up his spine—that ugly ball of emotion he had yet to process. He shoved it back down. "I used to visit her every day and—"

"Oh yeah, you're the mouse guy!" a guest interrupted, thrusting out her finger and nearly knocking a taxidermied rattlesnake off its pedestal.

Hudson tensed, but when he saw the woman smiling, he realized the comment had been one of friendly recognition, not accusation. He nodded before continuing his story. Still, relaxation proved difficult. While he spoke, he stumbled over his words, blinked rapidly, and picked at his thumbnail.

The tour ended thirty minutes later, and Hudson invited the group to roam the museum freely. Most stayed beside Alice as if she were an object of worship, possessing great power from beyond the grave. Trusting that no one would break anything, Hudson retreated to his office and shut the door. Away from the group and Alice, he could breathe more easily. Never in his life had he been a nervous tour guide. Even when he didn't know much about an exhibit, he'd always been able to confidently bullshit some talking points. He plopped into his swivel chair, closed his eyes, and rocked himself back and forth.

The tour group was gone when he emerged an hour later. Only Alice remained. Her golden eyes bore into Hudson's soul. He looked away. The taxidermist had replaced her real eyes with glass ones, but even those seemed too lifelike. It was hard to shake the feeling that some dark intelligence lingered behind them.

Night was fast approaching, the sky over the Platte River bruising purple. Nearly time for nocturnal predators to hunt, Alice among them.

Hudson shivered, then slapped himself on the cheek and laughed. Foolishness. He locked the museum doors and climbed the stairs to his loft bedroom. After the financial problems of the past year, he'd sold his home and converted part of the museum into a living space, figuring one mortgage would be a hell of a lot cheaper than two. Now he wished he could return to his old house— a place far from the museum and Alice's watchful eyes.

***

Hudson thought the egg was a joke. It was small and white with brown speckles, like any old bird egg. Maybe a museum guest had left it under Alice's display to be funny. But Hudson hadn't seen it there last night after closing the museum. Perhaps he'd been too tired to notice. After all, he hadn't been sleeping well.

The question of how the egg got there soon became less important than what he would do with it. Leaving it there was his first thought. The egg had fabulous narrative potential: "The Last of Her Kind and Her Unhatched Hope." But Hudson had already told his tour groups lies that left an ache in his gut; any further deception would give him stomach ulcers. The weight of all he'd done sank in accompanied by an unbearable quiet.

He picked up the delicate egg. His hand shook under its miniscule weight. His throat made sounds like painful swallowing and silent tears fell onto the shell. He gazed at Alice perched on the wall. She seemed to be looking at the egg.

"I'm sorry," Hudson said. His words were breathy and weak, on the verge of tears.

He rushed out the museum's front door, egg in hand, and greeted the punishing sunrise. It was April but felt like August. There was no breeze to grant him relief. Only the muggy, motionless air of the Platte River searing his lungs. He shuffled to the dumpster and gripped its edge, trembling.

"Goodbye," he said to the egg, then tossed it among the dozen black trash bags.

His vision stung. He breathed to bury the pain, each inhale and exhale another scoop of dirt atop its grave.

The sound of engines pulled him into the present. He pried himself from the dumpster and faced the caravan of vehicles kicking up dust from the country road. One by one, they pulled into the parking lot. This tour group looked even bigger than yesterday's.

Hudson took one final breath, forced a smile, and tried to forget all about the egg, all about Alice.

The show must go on.

***

With insomnia came hallucination. Or that's what Hudson prayed it was as he lay awake listening to the soft cooing downstairs. He refused to get out of bed and inspect. That would only give the psychosis more power over him. Pressing a pillow over his ears was the only rational solution. It reminded him of trying to sleep through a dying smoke alarm beeping at odd intervals. The cooing should have been easier to ignore than that, but every time he heard it, his spine stiffened and his hands clenched around the sheets like claws. He put a second pillow over his head to cocoon himself in silence, but the cooing grew closer the more he tried to shut it out: first at the foot of the stairs, then outside his bedroom door, and finally in the rafters above his bed. He ripped the pillows from his head and looked at the ceiling. Nothing. Not a roosting pigeon, not a misplaced mourning dove, not … her.

There was no chance he'd find sleep, so he pulled on a robe and shuffled to the bathroom. His bladder was half-empty when a massive metallic boom echoed outside the museum. In his panic, he pissed all over the wall and his robe, then quickly tucked away his penis. If a drunk driver had smashed into the museum, he'd have to catch them before they drove off. He dashed down the stairs, Alice's eyes burning into him as he passed her display case.

Even during a non-owl emergency, she made her simmering presence known. Hudson shook off the feeling, unlocked the front door, and ran into the parking lot.

In the darkness, there was no crumpled car smoking from the hood and leaking transmission fluid. No damage to the building either. Hudson wondered if the crash, like the cooing, had all been in his head.

Then he saw the tipped-over dumpster. Its torn plastic lid dangled like a hangnail and one of its wheels had broken off, bolts snapped clean in half. Somehow, no trash had spilled out when the dumpster fell, despite it being full. Hudson approached slowly. Whatever had done this could still be nearby. Only a car seemed capable of inflicting this much damage, but that explanation didn't make sense: the dumpster's dents jutted outward.

His mind strayed to Alice. To the egg. He breathed and tried to bury those thoughts under concrete instead of dirt this time, but they wouldn't go away. They would never go away.

Inching forward, he came to the dumpster's opening. Ignoring the inner voice screaming *no*, he bent down to look inside. The dumpster was empty. Or mostly empty. In the absence of sour, bulging trash bags, there was the egg, cracked in half. A viscous yellow goo lined the shell's rim.

Without another thought, Hudson ran back inside and locked the door behind him. He wouldn't come back out for another week.

***

Sick with something nasty, so the museum is temporarily closed, Hudson posted on social media. Will announce when tours resume! Peace, love, and conservation.

Countless replies of Get well soon! and How's Alice? and I traveled from New York to see Alice. You HAVE to reopen the museum NOW! flooded his notifications, but Hudson stared at his bedroom ceiling. He wanted to empty his mind of all thought.

Or, if that proved impossible, empty his veins of all blood. The morbid idea made him shiver. He pulled himself out of bed.

It had been a week since he'd left his room for anything other than a meal or a trip to the bathroom. Despite the April heatwave, he hadn't showered once. His sweat-soaked body smelled like parmesan cheese left out in the sun. Rather than worrying about hygiene, he worried about whatever was on the other side of his locked bedroom door. A few times each day and many times each night, something cooed from that other side and scratched the door three times. Always three. Hudson didn't sleep anymore, nor did he rest his eyes for long.

He couldn't hide in his room forever though. For the past three days, the fridge beside his bed had been empty save for an old bottle of ketchup, gummy around the lid. The hunger hadn't been so bad at first, but now it was a constant rumbling, knotting pain. Drivers wouldn't deliver this far out of town, so he'd have to go get food himself. That meant facing the thing behind the door, running down the stairs past Alice, and exiting into a bright, terrifying world haunted by … it. That thing in the egg. Hudson tried to convince himself that it had been a normal chicken egg and had nothing to do with the dumpster's damage, but purging his anxieties proved impossible.

Hunger pangs boiled his insides. He clutched his gut and took a deep breath. There would be no more avoiding it. He had to go out and get food. And really, what would be the point in coming back? He'd rent a motel room far away from all this. Take a goddamn shower. Wash away his filth and worries. Stay a while in some place that wasn't his home but felt infinitely more welcoming.

The promise of escape kicked him into action. He pulled on a T-shirt with armpit stains and some musky-smelling athletic shorts, grabbed his wallet and keys, and pressed his ear to the bedroom door. After a full minute of silence, he unlocked the door and dashed downstairs. Alice's gaze prickled the hair on his neck, but he couldn't bear to look at her. Never again. Maybe he'd give up the museum entirely, his mother's legacy be damned. Crying, he opened the front door. His tears glinted in the sunlight, a kaleidoscope of countless colors and emotions. He'd never felt this much all at once before. He'd never wanted to.

His car wasn't far off. He staggered toward it, legs zombielike after so many sleepless nights. The question of whether he'd be able to drive safely seemed important but not as important as getting away from the museum. Forward. Ten more steps to the car.

Then a shadow annihilated the sun. Too fast and dark to be a cloud, it hovered over Hudson and chilled the air around him. He didn't look up, didn't have to; he knew what it was. But he was so close now—to safety, a new life, and an unburdened mind.

Five more steps. A rush of beating arctic wind.

Four. A moan spilling from damned lips.

Three. A feathered midnight descending.

Two. Screams and prayers and failed burials.

One. Heavenward, heavenward, as the last of his kind.

ACKNOWLEDGEMENTS

First off, thank *you*, reader, for picking up *Extinction Hymns*. I hope it scared you, sickened you, punched you in the gut, and maybe made you laugh once or twice.

Thanks so much to everyone who helped me polish these stories for publication.

Thanks to Minicoven, my lovely writing group.

Thanks to the folks who originally published several of these stories: Scott J. Moses, *Starward Shadows Quarterly*, Dread Stone Press, Dark Dispatch, Jack Hartley, *Hyphen-Punk*, and Luke Kondor.

Thanks you, Elizabeth Leggett, for the spooky owl cover design.

Thank you, Heather and Steve at Brigids Gate Press, for believing in this book enough to publish it.

Thanks to my parents and sister for being always being loving and supportive.

And finally, thanks you, Kate, for being the best partner I could ask for. I love you deeply.

About the Author

Eric Raglin (he/him) is a Nebraskan speculative fiction writer and owner of Cursed Morsels Press. His debut short story collection is NIGHTMARE YEARNINGS, and his second collection, EXTINCTION HYMNS, is out December 2022. He is the editor of SHREDDED: A SPORTS AND FITNESS BODY HORROR ANTHOLOGY and ANTIFA SPLATTERPUNK. Find him at or on Twitter @ericraglin1992.

About the Illustrator

Elizabeth Leggett is a Hugo award-winning illustrator whose work focuses on soulful, human moments-in-time that combine ambiguous interpretation and curiosity with realism.

Much to her mother's dismay, she viewed her mother's white washed walls as perfectly good canvasses so she believes it is safe to say that she has been an artist her whole life! Her first published work was in the Halifax County Arts Council poetry and illustration collection. If she remembers correctly, she was not yet in double digits yet, but she might be wrong about that. Her first paying gig was painting other students' tennis shoes in high school.

In 2012, she ended a long fallow period by creating a full seventy-eight card tarot in a single year. From there, she transitioned into freelance illustration. Her clients represent a broad range of outlets, from multiple Hugo award winning Lightspeed Magazine to multiple Lambda Literary winner, Lethe Press. She was honored to be chosen to art direct both Women Destroy Fantasy and Queers Destroy Science Fiction, both under the Lightspeed banner.

Elizabeth, her husband, and their typically atypical cats, live in New Mexico. She suggests if you ever visit the state, look up. The skies are absolutely spectacular!

Content Warnings

Silver Dollar Eyes: child death by cancer

The Resurrection Doll: suicide, self-harm

Angel Teeth: drug addiction, torture

Transubstantiation: graphic child death

In His Youth: brief non-explicit mention of child sexual assault

A Most Bulbous Congregation: child torture, conversion therapy

The Last Summer: none

Elevator Boys: child death

Dead Rain: suicide, death of a parent, child death

A Coarse Yellow Sea: child endangerment and death, animal neglect, attempted suicide, internalized biphobia, homophobic language, spouse incarceration, drug use

What to Do with Grandpa: self-harm, dementia

A Creature Nailed upon the Corridor of Time: none

The Strangling Ash: mother death in childbirth, verbal and physical child abuse

Floaters: suicide, extreme violence, workplace misogyny

Boning: torture, extreme violence, cancer

Heirlooms: cancer, self-harm

'Til the Sun Wheel Turns No More: self-harm, extreme violence, parent rejecting gay child, Nazism

The Last of Her Kind: animal death

More from Brigids Gate Press

Betrayal brings grave ending to a noble bloodline. Forced to flee, its sole surviving heir is spared this fate by the timely intervention of a haunter of the wilds. In his charge, the maiden embraces the lore of the dark arts and rises to become the watch-keep of the woods. As decades pass, with her legend growing, the 'witch of root and earth' weaves subtle deceits in a tangled web of vengeance.

But will there be a fairy tale ending, or will poisoned legacies and pacts with dark forces see ambition unravel in her relentless pursuit of power?

Bloody, and brilliantly realised, Baird's dark fantasy nightmare spins a lavish tale of dread, desire, and fantastical fury.

A woman develops an unhealthy obsession with a scarecrow. A boy plays with a Ouija board and receives a terrifying warning of murder. A down-on-his-luck father learns what happens when you die in your sleep. These stories and six more frightening tales await the reader within the pages of Throwing Shadows: A Dark Collection.

Throwing Shadows will feed that hungry dark side that lives in your cellar.

During the Spring Equinox underneath London, four people enter the caves, but only one will survive. Each trespasser must battle their own demons before facing the White Lady who rises each year to feed on human flesh.

Return to the Weald, the world Stephanie Ellis introduced us to in The Five Turns of the Wheel.

Reborn is the story of Cernunnos, the Father of all, who has risen. Born of blood offerings, he travels to the Layerings—one of those places, like Umbra, which sit just beyond the human veil.

Reborn is the story of Tommy, Betty and Fiddler, the infamous troupe whose bloody rituals were halted by Megan, Tommy's Daughter. Rendered weak by Megan's refusal to allow them to hunt in the human world of the Weald, they seek their rebirth and forgiveness from the Mother and Cernunnos.

Reborn is the story of Megan, who follows Cernunnos and Hweol's sons on a pilgrimage of hope—one that would see her husband restored to her and the dark presence of Hweol removed.

Ultimately, though, Reborn is the story of Betty, the most monstrous of the three brothers. He is Nature, red in tooth and claw. He is what the Mother made him. And who are we to judge?

With Reborn, Ellis delivers another powerful tale of folk horror that will captivate the reader from the first page until its final bloody climax.

Visit our website at: www.brigidsgatepress.com